About the Author

Sam Smith started writing after facing unwanted challenges in her life, and her life path changed from working as an engineer to a writer. She tries to point out problems and issues that are mostly not seen in our busy routine life, but we are affected by their consequences.

New Year in Pandemic

تقدیم به آقای رضا کشی

سپاس اسدی

Sam Smith

sep 10, 2023

Sam Smith

New Year in Pandemic

Olympia Publishers
London

www.olympiapublishers.com
OLYMPIA PAPERBACK EDITION

Copyright © Sam Smith 2023

The right of Sam Smith to be identified as author of
this work has been asserted in accordance with sections 77 and 78 of
the Copyright, Designs and Patents Act 1988.

All Rights Reserved

No reproduction, copy or transmission of this publication
may be made without written permission.
No paragraph of this publication may be reproduced,
copied or transmitted save with the written permission of the publisher,
or in accordance with the provisions
of the Copyright Act 1956 (as amended).

Any person who commits any unauthorized act in relation to
this publication may be liable to criminal
prosecution and civil claims for damage.

A CIP catalogue record for this title is
available from the British Library.

ISBN: 978-1-80074-985-6

This is a work of author observation combined with fiction.
Names, characters, places and incidents originate from the writer's
imagination. Any resemblance to actual persons, living or dead, is
purely coincidental.

First Published in 2023

Olympia Publishers
Tallis House
2 Tallis Street
London
EC4Y 0AB

Printed in Great Britain

Acknowledgements

A special thanks to Olympia Commissioning Editor, James Houghton, for opening a door to the literary world for me and Olympia editor, Kristina Smith, who patiently worked on my book.

It is the last day of the year. We stayed home at least for last eight months. It is an epidemic in the city. At first, everyone was sacred, some people didn't come out of their home at all, some people were wearing strange coverage as if they were in a chemical environment. People were attacking stores to get groceries and their basic needs. All day you could hear from radio and TV news about this killing epidemic. Strange, seems this virus is all over the world. Borders are closed, schools, works, and almost every outdoor and indoor facility such as pools, gyms, and bars are closed. For some reason it wasn't real to me. I could see everyone's reactions but I couldn't believe it. In the twenty-first century, a world-wide virus couldn't be real, or because of a very hard life I had, this one looks nothing. Something inside my soul was telling me it is mostly a show or politics; not sure how, but I could feel it.

I knew sometimes you see evidences by your own eyes and acts are showing something, but you know deep down it's not true, and when you are listening to your instinct, you can clearly hear it says they are hiding the real truth. I guess because from the first step to that point, all are not in a row or on the right path. It is like solving an equation; you can see variables and constants but those operators are not working, even with replacing or changing them with all types of operators, this equation has some wrong parts and you can feel it but can't point it out.

Another fact during this exaggerating epidemic is some people are trying too hard to prove we are in danger, and worse than that, those authorities who usually in this situation try to calm people down are trying to make this fear and uncertainty situation even worse. I can understand an ordinary person's fears and concerns from unknown factors, but not those who know many facts behind the scene. Nothing makes sense. I have been trying to keep up with all types of limitations, bad news, and scared people, but based on what I experienced and studied. Even two hundred years ago, controlling epidemics didn't push people to fears, limitations, and isolation. They always are coming with consequences for generations and I don't understand why this year, we spent all our life being scared, isolated, and having conversations about who died or who is going to die, but this year is over, anyway. Good or bad, another year of my life is over and we start another year from tomorrow with millions of people living in uncertainty and an unclear future. They are pushed to live in a virtual world without contact and affections, which is scary. It is like we are moving from Earth to Mars, or another planet which contacting, touching or living in our normal situation will kill us.

I sit here alone thinking about what world would look like next year. In this year I was target of continuously testing like a mouse in a lab for what I listen, read, do, feel, or even how I sleep. When I think why I and other people were and are target of this strange testing, I think when a country is limited to staying home, not say hi to anyone, and just listen to specific news and information, those who are running these tests have a similar life to me, except they are aware of many hidden factors that make them smarter, and living in a dark and unknown environment makes me feel harassed by them.

I try very hard to put my feet in their shoes to see what they want from this situation, or what they are looking for. Continuous testing, doubting, and accusations. Then I got some results. When a person fails in what he should do the best, they try to cover it with blaming something or someone. The first thing that comes to their head is finding someone or some group to blame. If every single evidence and fact shows they cannot blame them, they try to find some out of control phenomena like epidemic, volcano, storm, or something we call - God acts. Those are the best excuses for covering lack of ability for managing what they are supposed to do the best. No one can blame disease or volcano or ask why no one makes it stop or manages them, but if you relate those failures to war, revolution, or other manageable factors, always someone will ask why you didn't stop it? Why couldn't you manage it? Why did you let it happen? Why do you ignore facts that are showing it is going to happen? And thousands of other questions.

So the creator of this unreasonable situation is looking for something which no one can question. First, targeting someone or some group seems a good idea but after a while truth comes out, and you can't target and blame them by following, spying and watching their every move and then creating some disaster for the country with relating consequences to their moves. That's why they have to look for something bigger than one person or a group's actions that doesn't need explanation, and the best excuse could be something like pandemic.

I am laughing now because it is too unrealistic to believe. The year is ended and millions of people are sitting in their home waiting for next year, and no one knows what is this or who creates this situation and still they try to cover up their failure to a target. In this moment I think how many years more we will sit in our home with all types of limitations, living in a virtual world, with closed borders and living in fear of unknowns and trying to find something that links this situation to that?

I remember I was studying many years ago about an upcoming world in which robots will take over human life and how we will live in virtual world. It was exciting at that moment, thinking about how technology will improve, like years of observing how black and white TV turned to watching your favorite movie or TV shows on your laptop or cell phone, but I never thought we would sit in our apartment with fear of seeing or contacting our friends and family, have an epidemic, and would wear masks and all types of covering for not getting this unknown disease and use the virtual world for our simple tasks.

Then it leads me to another thought: is this statement true? "It is not what it looks like." I think it might - it really is not what we see or what it looks like. It might be something behind this situation we can't see, or a group doesn't want us to see it. Personally, I try to believe that one. At least I don't feel stupid. This way, I push myself to believe we are living in a world where still smart people exist and managers know what they are doing and do not blame a target, or God acts for their failures. This way, I can start the new year with the hope we will stop living in a virtual world where no one knows which part is real, which part is not, and our kids won't be the result of lab experiments and adoptions without knowing who are their real parents.

Today is not like another day in my life. Today is a special day ending too many unwanted relationships, unrealistic thoughts and living in shadows, I want to believe today is the last day of living in lies and a fake world. I will start a new year tomorrow or even in a few minutes with a new reality, and new people who don't lie, don't fake it, don't pretend and don't want to stay in a blaming target world. I live with those who are free and don't hold others accountable for their mistakes. They accept their errors and try to fix it, don't put someone else's life on hold for their happiness. They are like me, tell the truth and live their life. I feel much better now. I end this whatever year with all uncertainty and lies and cover-ups. I am starting a new day and New Year.

For starting a new year, I try to recap my past year. It is somehow scary. I think, is it a way others lived, or was it just me? I am trying to find any new connection in the real world; someone I talked to and met in person, or hung out with for a while, or anything similar to my life before the pandemic, but in my head I just see smart TVs, cell phones, tablets, laptops and all types of conference video chats. I try to look for who I was talking to during this year but the only thing is coming to my head is Google assistance, Alexa and Bixby. Sounds scary, isn't it? We practically have been living in a virtual world for the last twelve months. I chat with my doctors, courts, lawyers, authorities and even my family in this world. I can't say all was bad; in many ways it was easier to have a video chat with someone when it was snowing, in rush hours, or when you were sick, rather than take a trip to meet them, but really was it what we forecasted for our life in the future? I remember I spent most of my childhood playing with kids even I didn't know on the street, or my teenage time visiting new places, eating in restaurants and coffee shops, watching movies in theaters and shopping all over the city. It might have had some discomfort but I was learning many things by interfering with others. Now we are all sitting in a bubble watching everything through our computers and virtual world eyes.

    I know there are many good things about sitting in your home and doing your work or connecting with someone regardless of where they are. Does it mean we are eliminating three dimensions of the world, or we are including those three dimensions in the fourth one which is virtual?

    I know it has been a long time since scientists were looking to make everything in four dimensions but I didn't think we were losing the rest. I was taught everything has its own definition based on two factors: time and place. If I can chat in the virtual world with another side of the world, I am eliminating location and somehow time. It could be good and bad. The good news is I am taking distance between by living in the virtual world, but the bad news is we are living in the same video conference room regardless of our culture, language, education, nationality, and even beliefs. At this point I think what does make difference between me and my roommate in the virtual world, for a while we will have small personal interest to talk, but if this virtual world continues nothing will remain. We both are sitting in our apartments talking to anyone and everywhere we like, and it is not any outside world I can learn or make me unique that I could explain to my roomy. We both are shopping online, visiting our doctors in video chats, and have a gathering online with strangers, our friends and family.

After a while, who can give a definition of family and friend? You, who is living on your computer and learning from someone else who lives on her cell phone, or I who just spends half an hour or max one hour to meet my virtual friends and families.

My family was unique when we had a chance to meet each other and every one of us could talk with her unique personality about her experience with her environment, age range, times and location, but what are we supposed to talk about now? We are living inside an apartment in a virtual world that after a while, nothing is left to talk about because nothing is going to happen outside. I can tell my kids or partner about how when I was cooking, I dropped a pan, or my kids can tell me how when they were on the computer, they got disconnected. There is no school, work office, driving, stopping in coffee shops, eating in restaurants or even hidden activities out of our room that we could keep as our secret with our best friend. We have to watch movies and news about what happened about those days when we were living in the real world, over and over, and after a while it will be nothing to talk about.

When we are not hanging out with anyone, obviously there won't be any fighting, disagreement or arguments. We simply can turn off our computers or leave the room. As a result, we don't need police, lawyers or courts. Good news is we are living very safe inside our apartment and on our computers. The bad news is we have all the time in the world to be depressed and get sick visiting doctors and specialists.

I noticed if you are driving and own a car you can go watch a movie or some places for fun without leaving your car. What is going to happen to those without cars or for our kids who spend all the time at home or inside a car without outdoor playing or experiencing the real world? Personally I am eating more since my laptop and smart TV are five meters from me and my cell phone is with me most of the time, even in my bed. I don't have anything else to do except to eat and live in virtual world. I even don't know if someone in my conference chat is real, or is in another version of virtual world, and it is already recorded to show he is there or listening, or is it a programmed robot who is chatting? It should be very easy; someone just lets a program run a show, answer or initiate a talk with you while showing a man or woman sitting on their computers or even eating something.

Is it what we were wishing for in our future? This way we won't feel anything soon. Our feelings will be disappeared quickly. We will forget what is love, hate, disappointment, anger or fear, because we are not experiencing them. We will turn to robots and our only differences with machines are gradually going out of the world.

This is what was predicted years ago, that robots are taking over our life. That's true. I can ask my Alexa to call, search and sing, or tell me a joke, and she knows better than everyone else what I like because she has access to my personal info and my interests.

I didn't attend any conferences and gatherings in person last year. I can get all the info on my smart TV or computers but who knows what is real what is not? I even heard you can listen to music and attend dancing events with video chats. Have we ever thought about why dancing, festivals, gatherings, or going to the mall is enjoyable? Isn't it because we are moving our bodies and they can work better and impact on our mental health, too? Meeting new adventures and people doesn't help us to learn more and feel more?

For a minute I am thinking about those years humans were living in caves and tents. They had a similar situation; it wasn't any car, factory, office, restaurant, coffee shops, theaters or malls. They were living together in one place, eating and learning in their small cave. They did not have any interference with others, not because of connecting by computer, but because they were scared of each other. It was a survival method; stay together as a small group and keep your foods and do not share with anyone. At first, when this pandemic started, people had the same survival method. They attacked groceries stores to get their necessary survival food and needs, and they were fighting with anyone on their way. Then it was an order to stay in small groups and do not share with others, exactly like cave living times. Later it expanded by virtual contacts. Thank God it is a small difference between the twenty-first century and cave living times.

In the past year we moved backward. I could see people are emotionally sensitive to anyone and anything like they are all on a mission to fight for living with their virtual friends, and in some cases with their virtual partners and foods. Staying inside for a long time is just like living in hospitals or nursing homes because of your health, but at least those know they do not have other options. Living in small groups and ready to fight for survival reminds me of those who are held in prison.

In anyway, this year is over and we will start another year soon in less than thirty-six hours. I am living on my computer just like millions of people and spending the countdown in a virtual world which no one knows is from this year or is recorded before. It is a New Year and new life. I am trying to find predictions for this upcoming year to see what will be different from the fake year we lived.

Yep, it is a new year. We already started it six days ago in the virtual world with time differences where no one knew we had already passed the ball dropping moment, or what we were doing in turning last year to New Year time. Somehow it was funny on another side of world; they started almost one to two days before us and we were watching something we thought was a New Year celebration. I tried to find the exact time of the New Year in my area but it wasn't possible because news was coming from all over the world and my receiver was showing the first launch footage. I guess personally I heard three countdowns from three different areas. I didn't understand which one was real or in my area but we started this year with a few variations around a minute to two days.

Since the first day of the New Year, we keep hearing we should stay home and not plan any outside activities and even shopping. Those warnings make me think this is not a real pandemic, it is something related to closing borders which if you think deeper make sense somehow. Are they thinking what I think? If we are going to open our borders like a global village and live with everyone's culture, religion, language, and of course politics, sooner or later someone or some area starts expanding his territory under unity and globalization and it would be too late to save this area or that area. I don't know if I should be sad or happy because in that situation it won't be any war where someone can take over other territories in peace and slowly move to each other's borders and cultures. The sad part is no one could know who is enemy and who is friend, or who should get reward or be punished. This movement is smart, slow and dangerous. At this moment, I think isn't this the life we have been living for years? Those who planned and were real trouble makers were rewarded and those who tried to warn and stop this wave were punished? How about this pandemic and staying home and not connecting with anyone or anything? For some reason I am getting a headache thinking about this. I need to clean my head and then rethink. The situation is more critical than what I can think of in a few minutes.

Another week passed with the same situation and living either with a few family members or just on the computer and smart technology. I am thinking I might sit on my couch in my apartment next year and still ask what is happening to the world, or why I can't understand my own kids, family and friends. I am sure in that time, many other groups already turned to robots and prefer to sit in their apartment and play online, talk and have fun in their virtual room and do other aspects of life. I won't able to say hi to them if I see them on the street. Wait a minute - will any walking on the street exist in the next year? Or are we eliminating anything outside our apartments because we need to stay safe? It is like we are melting in movies online to become part of the time was a real world to make a movie out of it. Does it mean we are traveling to old times? It makes me for a moment feel I am blocked in a black box with no hope to have a real life. I am part of old living life which I miss deeply; having relationships, family, job, party, travel and real conversation with real people. I don't know if it's called safety or fear, but I feel those black box walls are coming closer to me and making it difficult to breathe. It is like I was put inside my coffin while I am alive, and my scream is not heard. It is like Alice in Wonderland; either they are not real, or they are exaggerating real things. Is that the reason my teapot is bigger than usual? Or can I put my cell phone in my coffee cup like that rabbit in wonderland? For ten seconds I felt lost, not sure if it was a dream world or living in a coffin.

There was a time when I wished I had robot assistance or was working from home instead of leaving my warm apartment in cold weather or watching my family from this side of the world. Wow, is it the meaning of my wish coming true? I have to make sure I am not wishing for anything else or thinking about my wishes. If I wish to be a millionaire and it comes true, it has millions of consequences. Okay, now I feel much better to know not every wish comes true. I try to find some positive sides to this situation. If I am Alice and it is Wonderland, I can talk with everything inside my apartment like my TV, lights, security camera, or even my oven. At this moment I realize I am living in Wonderland. If it was a dream one day, today is real, and I can talk to them and they are responding. When did I fall down in that hole which I can't remember? When I was playing on the ground, or the time I was driving to my work office, or it might be the time I was taking my kids to school, how come no one noticed there was a hole in the ground that is linked to another world? I remember I had read somewhere there is a hole in Earth, or even there is a Bermuda Triangle which whoever passes could fall in and disappear. Oh my god, we are disappeared. We are in that hole. That's why no one can find us and no one is trying. We should all get back to the ground exactly like Alice who was escaping from evils and looking for a way to get back to her real life. I guess we all should find that rabbit or believe we are the only ones who can help us, and don't wait for any rescue groups. They are not stepping in Bermuda holes. Take a minute to look around my apartment. I can see a table with food on it, some devices, furniture and teapot which I can talk to and that's it, nothing more.

It is a door that is supposed to be an escape way to outside but there is nothing there. The street dead last year and then everything after that, one by one. I used to walk to the coffee shop close to my home just to interfere with humans but recently they all closed. What is the point of this door? A door that opens to nowhere. We should find a way to get out of this underground tunnel. We need to contact and communicate. We should exchange our thoughts with someone real, not just some devices. Again I get back to the virtual world, somehow, and suddenly this world looks much better than before, because it is our only option. What is this epidemic which makes us accept the fear of living in Wonderland or Bermuda instead of accepting the fear of getting sick?

I read about those who got lost in Bermuda. After a while searching rescue groups give up and go after their life. After a few years their memories and their lost stories is in the news and then are forgotten. No one even thinks they might be alive. They chose to believe they are dead and there is no way to rescue them. In that side they are doing everything to contact the outside world and wait for help, first with everything that remained from their broken ships, planes, trains or anything that got them to that mess. After all their attempts fail, they start to use old ways like lighting a fire or writing SOS on beaches or shooting their last bullet, and then they try to adopt a new life. They have a little hope but try to make the best of what they have? Not the best of what they lost.

After surviving they are ready to attack anything and everyone to protect their left overs. They are angry to notice everyone forgot about them. They remember those who kept telling them how much they are loved, and those who they loved and were ready do anything for them. For a few years they live with their memories and then they change. There is no way out. They are adopting new basic living with whatever they can make for themselves. Their lifestyle changes from whatever they had before to a new possible living and their dreams change from having a bigger better house, car and job to one day getting back to civilization. I hear a bell is ringing in my ears and ask, is it what we should expect from this epidemic situation?

I try to look back from the beginning of pandemic. Yes, that is exactly what happened. We all sit in our home waiting for someone to save us. We were counting minutes to see when we were told it was over, we are free get back to our normal life. Suddenly we were jubilant with everything we had or had not before, even if we thought they were disasters before; our friends who we barely contacted turned to our newly friends. After a few months when we noticed this epidemic might continue for a long time, we started to forgive our enemies and ask God forgive us for what we did or did not do. We tried to be more understanding to those who remained for us and even though we weren't close to them before, we accepted they were the best we had. It happened gradually; we didn't notice how we turned from our previous version to this version. We followed the news and asked each other what is recent news, but the only news was the number of deaths and how to live isolated if you want to stay alive.

Before we were very serious about how our kids talk or behave, or their education, but it changed to being happy they are alive. If anyone sneezes or coughs we accuse him of spreading the virus. We didn't wear makeup or fix our hair. We were alive and it was enough for wearing a mask and covering ourselves, for not contacting this unknown disease. Following that, businesses were closed, we didn't shop, did not wear perfume or go to the theatre. We didn't do exercise to stay fit or go to the beach to get a tan. Our only thought was eating and visiting a doctor. Everything outside that was irrelevant. We were happy, we are inside home and had food to feed our family and this was the best thing that has happened to us for long time. If anyone expects more, accuse him of not understanding, being selfish and not considerate. We eliminated our celebration, gathering outside and traveling.

Businesses started to make losses instead of gains and it made them reduce their personnel and hours. As a result, many lost their jobs but still we were happy, we were alive and no matter what we were receiving government assistance to survive. Our kids from active, wild and curious changed to moms, dads; kids who we should take care of them inside our home without putting them in danger, and they have to adopt living inside small or big spaces with their sisters and brothers, or in some cases with step-siblings regardless of their age differences or life styles.

During all those transfers, we thought we were doing great managing the critical situation and keeping our loved one alive. No one saw how we were changing, how we were fighting for whatever was very basic in our previous life. No one understood those who expected more than the basics, trying to keep their lifestyle matched with the advanced century. We take them down and are proud of what we were doing. Food and medication were what we needed and nothing more. We decided and picked this life. Why are we waiting for changes or looking for someone to rescue us? Those who had family stuck with them and those who were singles were scared to get this whatever disease and kept themselves away from any contact, and then after one year passed, they expected a magical power or supernatural to save them, but the truth is, we fell down into that hole and didn't even notice.

In similar situations, usually it is one or a few persons trying to take responsibility and manage others. They sacrifice some of their needs to help others but they are stories in movies. Not sure in the real world anyone was or is ready to take responsibility. Isn't the reason this situation was linked to not predicted, without control epidemic? We sat in our home and watched everything we had built going down and didn't try to save it. We were scared if we try, we'd be labeled as not understanding and careless. We thought, if like everyone else, we feel sorry for ourselves and wait for some outside power to save us, we'd belong to this desperate population, and it is brave to attack anyone and say something against this approach. We became our family God, who had created our kids and now had power to control and save them by keeping them inside and taking them to doctors and hospitals and make them stay away from those who are doing anything except that. Our family and others were cheering for us and we turned to hero, but we didn't realize how we were losing our identity and living style. It happened slowly when we were busy taking possible danger away. We all in Wonderland playing with our exaggerated house stuff and were talking through the virtual world. Suddenly it was looking great to sit at home and do whatever you wanted in your time schedule without any supervision, limitation or even specific area. It was a new world and we all excited like a kid with a new toy.

At first we were talking to one person at a time and later we learned to have a conference video chat. We were showing our next generation how smart we are and could keep everyone connected with family and friends without even moving. We were getting very good in this virtual world and improved ourselves the way we did not even need to take a shower, sit, or even change our PJs. We could manage all those conferences in our bed and in our PJs, it was improvement and one step further than we had learned before. As a result of this new method, we were paying less bills for utilities, transportation and parties, and somehow we found ourselves successful in managing our finances and every time proudly show our bills to our partners and told them how we are able to control every situation, even in emergency and disaster. After a while, if any bill was a few dollars more than what we had paid in the last month because our kids took showers or our partner had bought a new lotion, it was an argument followed by a fight, warning them how they are wasting money for unnecessary materials and emphasizing how we have to keep our money for food and medicine, nothing else.

Kids gradually turned to couch potatoes, sitting in their PJs many times without cleaning their ears or faces and were playing video games or watching new movies, and we were very happy to see they were not going outside or asking more than what they have, and we don't have to buy them clothes, cosmetics or take them to movie theaters or playgrounds. We were already living in Wonderland and our teapot was talking and a rabbit was sitting in our coffee cup. We did not need anything else.

After the first six months, if we saw anyone cleaned and dressed up, we thought he must have found a cure for this virus or his life is completely different from us. Then we turned to his enemy and tried to find out what is in his life which makes him still, after spreading this deadly disease, dressing up and perhaps smile. After spending a period of time comparing his life with our life, we started to create new theories. He must have some connection out of this environment, or receiving some rewards from outside governments, or he is this disease main reason in the first place, and thousands of other theories that made us be happy with ourselves and gave us excuses for being sad, demanding and angry, they were some type of peace of mind for us, and in another hand we could prove to our subsidiaries and families it is not our problem, we are managing the best we could. If they saw someone living in a different way, we expected and accepted there must be a dangerous reason behind it, and this way we kept our family satisfied.

It is like a tree's root that spreads inside soil, this type of living spread under our values and principles and our kids learned to make targets from anyone who is against this living style or what they were taught is right. We even started using our left hand less because in Wonderland, using the left hand is not right, exactly like hundreds of years ago when anyone using his left hand was punished, and they made him just use his right hand. This harassment was used by teachers and parents because they thought they didn't want their kids to be different, or as this day's kids say, being a freak. We got back to those years in which everything should be right and based on what we define, and anyone who does not obey is evil and does not belong to our living environment. This culture grew in our society and anyone who said something we didn't like, we made a group to attack him exactly like thousands of years ago, which for defending what we are doing right, we sent our men to fight. This time we taught our boys and men should fight too and keep background fighters, which included women and kids safe, with a little difference. This time, women were leading their men to fight their competitors and those who are threatening their kids, but the similarity was, after every attack, men and women took whatever remained for their wealth, then we were running to our home to celebrate our victory with what we gained and were telling stories about how our enemy failed and our kids and family were cheering for us. We spent almost all year with this hobby and didn't realize that in Wonderland, there is not any winner or loser. We all fell down in that hole sometime during this process; some sooner, some later. Like Bermuda survivors we started to build new homes, which compared with what we had, was a shelter, but we were very proud that in this situation we were able to do that. Slowly, our foods and water were going out of stock, but that was no problem at all. We could take care of that, too. We started to hunt and find any fruit or even grass which could keep us alive. It didn't matter if we had to cross others territories, or if it was necessary even to kill them. At first, we were hunting small things, or sometimes stealing them, but later we were highly skilled in this hunt and taught our kids to go hunting and be brave and not scared of war, compromise, or even spy on others. Kids were fast learners and they could improve their skills quickly.

It wasn't any mercy or sympathy they had survived for a long time, and for being alive, they would do whatever they could. We and everything around us were melting in this survival method and theories the way we completely forgot what our basic living style was before that. In the morning families were getting up early or late, it didn't matter any more. Sometimes they changed their clothes, sometimes not, but what was important listening to news about this killing virus and what they should eat and how prepared their necessary gradient, and after that were being busy for another night and sleeping and getting up tomorrow with the same routine.

During the year 2020 we learned to live like our past generation, but since we were in Wonderland and they weren't, we found the virtual world and became part of that. We could jump inside any chat room and chat without knowing whether they are real or not, but still we were very happy compared to past generations. They weren't that smart to create a virtual world, so in this point, we sat on our couch no matter how and started to talk to someone who his thoughts are exactly similar to our thoughts, and if anyone says something we didn't like, the same elimination method could be performed in this world, too. Either we kick him out of the gathering or simply eliminate his access and remind ourselves we are right and not left and no one should say anything we don't like. During these eliminations and sending out, we made sure to prove that anyone who has different appearances or still smile or is not messed up is dangerous and shouldn't be in our important right gatherings, and this method of eliminating melted gradually in our culture too and made us be very proud and safe.

After New Year's Eve, I tried this virtual world for two months more since this was the only way for contacting outside our box. It was an interesting experience; we all were scared of each other to talk or make a conversation. It was identical to the real world. They are always people ready to judge you. If you say nothing, you are hiding something, or are there just to spy on them. If you be friendly and chatty, you have a plan for monitoring what they say and use it against them. If you look good, there are those who think you have absolutely no problem in your life because even in these pandemic times you changed and fixed your hair. If you look messy and careless, it means you didn't want to be here and it is a sign of objection to politician strategy for keeping you inside. If you smile, immediately, some copy you the way you look stupid who in this disaster situation are smiling, then they question you in their head: are you happy that we are isolated? It's like they are the only ones who are in this situation. If your face shows no emotion it means you are not having fun. Then why are you here? If you attend local virtual meetings, it definitely is a sign that you are here to get secrets information locally, which apparently they know and you don't. If you attend international gatherings, suddenly all conversations turn to a conservative version because who knows, you might be president of X country and are wearing a mask. After all, depends on every meeting subject, you are under question. What was in your mind that you picked this or that, and this goes on and on and on.

After a few meetings in this new year, I realized in the real world we could stick with a few gatherings that are in our interest, and I guess after a few times attending, we believed we all have something in common to pick this, but in the virtual world we have this chance to attend every meeting we like, then if other attendees don't know you, this is a big alarm. I thought, how come we can't trust each other? Is it something about what we discussed in meetings or what we experienced in time we are trusted, or do we prefer to have a virtual meeting with those who wear, talk, and their appearances are like us? This way we know they are part of our objection groups, or are here to have fun, or are taking steps further and get to personal info and relationships.

I noticed in one meeting which I used to attend in person, attendees were showing lots of attitudes like they are from Mars and I am from Earth. At this moment I can hear my laughing loud. Something we still did not understand was we all fell down in the hole and are in Bermuda years before this pandemic, and still they are looking for someone to blame. I didn't understand why we just can't stay with God's act and cover all our failures and anger under this, instead of looking to find a victim take our anger on her?

When we all are living in Bermuda, why are you trying to pretend what you did or do wrongly is a mirror of someone else, or try to prove you are good and someone else is bad? I know in some cases in court jury committees and judges try to recreate crime scenes to find out who is at fault, but something I didn't understand is why in this virtual world, still we try to recreate our wrong doing to blame someone else?

I guess we started a new sabotaging method in the virtual world in 2021. Now that we all are isolated and have to live on our computers, cell phones, and new technologies, it is the best time for turning the table. In real world, usually those who are more sporty, socialize more, or are good in making conversation are popular and those who are shy, don't like to attend gatherings, and mostly are very smart and computer oriented are victim. In the virtual world, they are taking revenge, and by taking over new technology made decisions about who can come inside their chatroom and who doesn't. Besides, they can stop, run, and even eliminate any rooms if they don't like it. That's why you better be careful how you present yourself in the virtual world.

However, we are sitting in our apartment, and from the comfort of our home talking, writing and chatting, but the reality behind who we are didn't change. Always there are those who blindly obey and there are those who are show runners. They are who direct the first person in a row to be blindfolded by someone behind him and it repeats to the end of the row. This way no one can see the truth and they are led to what they are supposed to see and understand. The difference between this new world and the old world is when you are sitting in your comfort zone, you prefer to be directed to not risky tasks and accept anything you are told, even when you know it's not true and are accusations because you like to stay in your comfort zone. But in the old world we were facing different angles of life and sometimes we felt it worth the risk of going out of our comfort zone.

However, it doesn't matter anymore. We are in Bermuda and Wonderland without even knowing it and still try to control and accuse a person whose appearance or ideas are not like us. This way there is no hope for finding the rabbit or exiting from this world because we prefer to be in our comfort zone and stay with the group that likes us, not that person who is not obeying all the time and is not blindfolded.

A few days after my last writing, surprisingly, news announced some areas and businesses are reopened with limited capacity. In some locations, people were happy and screaming for this achievement like they won Nobel prizes for making world peace. It was exactly what was expected when you are in an underground Wonderland for a long time. Even having a cup of coffee with rabbits looks good and enjoyable. It is what we are making out of rebuilding downgrade life. Before we were fighting with our kids for not going outside and staying with their computer and TV inside their room, but suddenly we are celebrating our kids could go to shopping malls or restaurants with a limited capacity. In our old world, we could get lost in the crowd on the subway or at parties, or even in big square in the middle of city and not be seen by our unwanted followers, friends, or simply feeling good not be different from others but after taking this simple joy out of our life and living in Bermuda, getting a quarter of this access is a victory and we are very happy to let our family and friends know we are allowed to go out for a limited time and access the basic.

    For some reason we didn't control our family for doing their homework, jobs and responsibility because we felt they might be under stress in Wonderland and this exit door finally could open in somewhere. However, compared to what we had, it is tiny opportunity. During these isolation periods we learned talking to someone in person or hearing news from an old friend is valuable, and then we improved ourselves from sitting on our coach to going out of our box slowly and of course safely.

We were very excited and couldn't hide our happiness for this basic access, and as soon as we stepped out of our box with all hopes faced with a few people who wear masks and a street that was dead, quiet and creepy, we walked to our favorite places, but everything had changed. A few stores were open and a long line up in front of them and people stood with distance and covering their faces. They were places we used to go and touch someone's hand or shoulder to ask him what is the time, or get directions, or even ask how much they paid for their hats or shirts, but this time was different. Everyone was happy because we were out of exit door and were seeing others but our emotions were changed from joy and having fun to conscious and monitoring who has symptoms. We didn't care if stores had sales or new fashions. Standing in a long line up after a long time in isolation wasn't any fun, it was just another version of following the rabbit and buying some tea cup for getting back to our underground Wonderland. We got back home tired but satisfied we got some of our basic needs, which before weren't even important, and prayed this limited access remain for at least a few weeks and will not be taken from us. In the meanwhile, we put our kettles on oven and made a pot of tea to feel we are still alive and could drink our tea without interruption by rabbits.

At first, while we were scared, we still had some expectations from our living environment, but they were replaced with our basic needs gradually, the way even we didn't notice why talking to someone became an important factor in our life, or having a conversation in the virtual world about some nonsense subjects made us satisfied and happy. Our options turned from all types of necessary and luxury to just surviving needs. We used to pick property for our living with some access to swimming pools, stores, gyms and libraries, but in this isolation we just wanted to have a place to live with our family inside, no matter how small or elementary it was. Just being safe was valuable.

Before we had invitations for several parties and we were thinking how annoying it is we are invited to attend to not interested meetings. We were busy with traveling, family and business gatherings and parties and didn't have time to pay attention to X or Y's request for going to a coffee shop, but in the new world, we were sitting for a long time in front of computers and cell phones, hoping someone would call or ask us to attend, at least in their virtual parties. While we passed 2020 and moved to 2021 even this expectation looks too much, because they were a group who had this chance to eliminate others and then cover it with computer errors. While we were in this underground life that is moving to a smaller world. That's why our borders were closed and capacities were limited. Our dinner table got longer and our dishes increased. We saw rabbits are jumping from this side to that side, but humans are sitting on long dinner tables, and after, eating a large plate of food, talking to dishes and teapots.

I used to think the month of January is longest month of the year because after Christmas, I have to pay my bills with money I already had spent for Christmas celebrations and gifts, but months in 2021 look shorter, because after half an hour attending virtual meeting and talking on the phone with someone who has nothing to say except pandemic news, which we are hearing all day long over and over, we had all day to eat and sleep. We didn't feel time passing and our life is flying on. Before I was counting days for getting to Friday and Saturday, which was party night and rest day, or doing what I didn't have time to do before, but in this pandemic, I even didn't know which day of the week it is. The door to outside was closed. I am on my coach and food is ready. Who cares if it is November 2020 or Feb 2021? In either way, we can't feel outside weather or life. I know in some parts of the world; six months are nights and six months are days. I had questioned myself how someone could live in this situation in which you don't know when to go to bed. It doesn't matter - six hours or fifteen hours, you never could know when another day is. There isn't any sunrise or sunset. It was very scary but now we are living in this world where, no matter if it's summer or winter, cold or hot, we are inside our box and apparently it is a good sign of being alive.

We almost are in the third month of the New Year, but absolutely no difference from last July, October, or December. The same repetitive life. We are waking up, eating, spending a few hours with Alexa, Bixby and Google assistance and sleep. For some reason, even someone visiting us is not as enjoyable as before. We try to pretend we are okay and live normally, and our feelings are the same as before, but we all know they are not. During last year's March to this year's March we used to live alone, isolated, and on our computer. We lost our feeling for laughter, joy, and heart-warming. We observed how we were eliminated for our accents, races, and living styles. We were asking ourselves why we should hang out under discrimination and stereotyping when we could stay in boxes safely.

Unlike those for whom given limited access makes them happy, some of us thought, what is the point of going outside in an environment where most people are cold and are ready to do anything to live a better life than you, even by pushing you out or replacing you? We thought, at least in my virtual world of computers and cell phones we are obeying programmers and don't make decisions on the spot out of being selfish or racist, and this way, month after month passed and we were still sitting on our couch remembering those things we had that were taken.

Two days ago, after a long time talking to my teapot and my imaginary rabbit in Wonderland, I tried to exit from this door that opens to nowhere. I was debating whether I should try it or stay safe. I walked in my six-hundred square feet apartment back and forth thinking. I sat for a while and thought about all the problems that might occur if I stepped out of my apartment, then I stood up and looked outside my building through my window. Everywhere was quiet and a few brave men and women were wearing masks and running to their cars. Some of them didn't go too far to make sure that if someone sneezed or coughed they could get back inside and be safe. It took half of the day for me to decide if I should take this risk and go outside, or stay in. Finally, I felt very brave, changed my PJs, which were on me for the last three days, and even didn't wash my hair because under hat and mask, there was no need for it. I slowly walked to my exit door and for thirty seconds. I kept the door handle in my hand. It was one of the best moments in my life, going out of this lonely box, the excitement of taking fresh air in my lungs and perhaps facing a human, but I released it fast, thinking, what if no one is outside? What if this last year living in my apartment, and not feeling love or pleasure, would kill me if I feel something? What if those I knew before this pandemic are dead and I watched their recorded clips and voices in virtual worlds? What if the world outside changed and I didn't know anything about it? I came back to my couch and sat, put my hands on both side of my chicks, and told myself safety is important and I have to be careful. After another half an hour, and nothing to do while I was in my outside outfit with my gloves, mask and hat, I turned the TV on again and got lost in the virtual world.

It took hours for me to find out where I was, and when I tried to look outside to see if still I could go outside and exit the door bravely, it was too late, it was dark, and not even a bug was flying. I walked for ten meters to my bedroom, changed my clothes, and went back to my couch, happy I didn't have to sanitize my clothes, hands, and everything I thought was touched by the outside world, and I could eat and drink tea. Now it was obvious why in Wonderland, there are lots of fruits, foods, and plants. I opened the fridge door and ate again and again, thinking another day had passed and it is sleep time. I might be brave enough to go out of my room and buy some groceries. I laughed. Suddenly, groceries looked so exciting and happy hours. I was very sure something happened to our three-dimensional world last year and we somehow moved to the fourth dimension. That's why I couldn't understand what is happening.

The day after I decided to go out and find a way to normal life, I walked to the door, and after lots of effort and inside fighting, I finally opened it and stepped out of my apartment. The corridor was dead, even unlike before I could see some trace of garbage on the floor. Close to the elevator was a post on the wall saying to stay away from each other and do not occupy the elevator with more than three, but amazingly, this post looked old, like it was on the wall for years. The paper was like it was left under rain and their tapes were all over the place. During the waiting time for reaching the elevator, I thought about how long we were in Wonderland, that it looked a decade. The elevator door was opened and I stepped in. A huge post inside was warning of wearing masks even in the common area. I thought, but no one is in the common area, anyway, and I saw in the elevator mirror I was smiling. The ground floor wasn't better than my floor, every security person was hidden behind a big mask, and in the front of front desk, a glass wall was grown. In my head, I really believed I was in my apartment for a century, and during that period, everything was changed. I tried to check on our swimming pool and gym, but all doors were closed with a big post saying, "Do not touch the door and stay away from any facility." I remembered it was a time we used to say hi to front desks people and even hold the door for anyone behind us, but this time we weren't allowed to look at each other. It was a big sign of danger, or probably symptoms of the virus, so I kept my head down and with caution, pushed the door to the outside area without knowing what was waiting for me. Based on what I had been hearing, it was a huge risk to step out of your home, and it might kill you. Interesting, I never understood what this virus was. I doubt if even doctors knew, but anyway, I was in front of a door that could be the only door to outside the building, and I already had pushed the button. For a minute, I stopped and thought it couldn't be the only door. I had seen before in emergency times, there are other doors we could use, and why am I picking this one? I waited there to see who else, if anyone, is going out of this door. There was a scary silence on the ground floor. I released the button and walked to the glass window to see if anyone was showing virus symptoms outside, but no one was there. I turned my head back to see if our front desk people were showing any motion, but it was impossible. You could see them through a glass wall, and tones of packages which had not been delivered at unit doors since the beginning of this epidemic had blocked the view. For a few minutes, I stopped there and reviewed all the bad and scary news I had heard during the last year. I tried to find something to be a bit positive, but whatever came to my head was "stay home", "do not touch anything", "stay away from each other", "stop going outside for unnecessary activity", and of course, death and death and those who are in hospitals with horrible symptoms. It means if I step out, I will die. For some reason, I walked to the only chair in our lobby that wasn't taken after this epidemic, sat there, and tried to breathe. I thought I could go back to my apartment and stay there, but then thought how, if ever, this situation would end. We will gain weight and even we couldn't pass through our door and no one would come to save us. Slowly, I stood up again, walked to the same door, and this time pushed the button fast and ran out of the door. No one was around, but the same news and posts were everywhere. It was like they were pointing at you for their mistakes. While I was passing the front building area, suddenly I noticed a person was coming from another side to my face. I thought, didn't you listen to the news? Didn't you hear this virus is killing us? But it looked like he was doing it on purpose because the same groups who by negligence let this happen, and then blamed God and let anyone think it was and is in God's hands now, has to target someone in case someone gets sick. No one questions their safety protocol or asks them why your plan didn't work, so it is better he comes to my face, just in case, for future reference.

I wasn't sure it was real or another cover up for negligence, but since I was going to die soon because of not staying home and stepping out of the door, I just changed my line and crossed the street to another side. This adventure took around ten to twenty minutes. However, a few people were around, but the way they were acting was like they were threatening you are responsible if something is going to happen, or perhaps for why it started in the first place. While I was coming back, I thought one year had passed and still we are looking for a victim to blame for not taking care of our responsibility. In this Wonderland that we all fell down in the hole, still finding someone to put all fault on her was our biggest power? For how long will we blame God for this situation or try to point at a victim to make themselves good? Who knows? It might take a long, long time, and as long as we are isolated in our apartment or living in a virtual world, we even don't understand we already lost three dimensions of our life. Pushing the button for entrance was like stepping on the moon, a big victory. I could go outside and came back in the pandemic. I was very proud of myself for doing this incredible adventure walking twenty minutes around my home, and the best part, I was home safely.

Days after days passed, listening to news and moving to another channel didn't change anything. We all hide behind our masks looking for someone to blame or save us. We thought if we could find someone to take responsibility for this pandemic we would feel better, as a result news could expand from just talking about the virus and finding a vaccine to attacking a person or a group. We remembered many times hearing on radio and TV when it was bombing, a group of terrorists had taken responsibility, and then we were relieved to know how badly they would be punished, but this time, not masking, sanitizing, or even hospitalizing wasn't any help to transfer responsibility to anyone, and we were very disappointed.

After a few weeks suddenly some good news spread in the city, in which some areas with color coding was opened. We jumped out of our isolation area and ran to the malls and streets to see what was new, but it was another instance of checking your temperatures, asking for health checks and lining up everywhere. I don't know it was the excitement of finding some exit door to the outside, or staying a long, long time inside my apartment, or if it was symptoms of standing in a line up and answering health questions over and over, but after ten minutes I couldn't walk, or even stand. I sat in the middle of the mall with yellow tapes around, exhausted. I could categorize people in a variety of groups; a group who couldn't stay in their skins for prison break, a group who used to run in front of others in crowds without considering their personal spaces, a group who this epidemic made them slow because they knew there wasn't any other activity around. A group who were jumping on buying whatever they could to make sure, if they had to stay in isolation for another year, they would have anything they needed. A group who were scared even to look at others to protect themselves from the killing virus, and this list was going on and on, but something they all had in common was that they all had worn masks, nobody knew who was really behind them. They will all get back to their homes and will stay there for another waiting period.

When I came back home, I thought, at least I could discover another part of Wonderland. Since the weather is getting better, I remembered my birthday last year, It was at the peak of this epidemic and I just, like anyone else, had thought, if not on the day I was born, but at least next month, I could celebrate my birthday in some restaurant, or travel somewhere, but a year passed and my birthday celebration never happened. I saw many video clips of people in their PJs on their birthday, by making some funny video, were trying to just get over this fact that they had to stay at home and not go anywhere or touch anyone, not even a friendly hug. In this moment, again my thoughts got back to Bermuda, the place where we build a new life and are happy, are making our basics, like going out of our tree house for our birthday to celebrate with coconut and banana with our neighbors who we don't like, and were fighting with them for saving our foods and whatever remained from our past life.

Interesting, this staying home somehow killed my excitement for adventure and curiosity. I guess my brain got used to living in a comfort zone with my computerized friends. It was easier to talk to Alexa and Bixby rather than my friend who preferred to spend a few allowed hours walking outside with someone else than me. This way, if Alexa doesn't understand my feelings with nonsense answers, she at least makes me laugh, or if Bixby instead on singing a song, or giving me a list of websites with song words, gives me sorry I don't understand this, I knew it was not intentional, it was just an error, but how can I convince myself when my friends ignore my feelings, or lie, or hide something from me that it is intentional? Then I thought, isn't this the definition of "bright side"? When we know it is a bad situation and we are stuck, try to cover it with a "bright side" phrase? Why do we use "bright"? Does it mean we are stuck in the dark? Or hoping that a bright point in our life makes us survive by finding something to hang on to? In either way, regardless of dark or bright sides, I missed my birthday, and my brain chose a comfort zone over taking risks which I was not sure were good or bad.

After a long time staying home, I decided for another time to step out and pushed myself to change and go out to take care of some financial issues. To me, it was something I should have done after one year staying home, but I didn't know I was doing the worst crime on the world. As soon as I stepped out of that exit door, it was like I was stealing other people's lives in underground tunnels and Wonderland, and this exit door never should have existed in the first place. I faced with faces were asking Why, while they are in their PJs without showers, and perhaps are sneezing, am I allowed to go outside and take care of unnecessary matters like finance? They tried to show and remind me it is Wonderland and we live underground. As long as they don't need any money or have any financial issue, I have to stay inside too, and live with their fear and isolation. Their face mimicry searching in my heart to find why in this disaster I am doing my finances rather than love them, or feel their fears. In my brain, they were looking for either stupidity, or a piece of my brain to give them a solution for their problems in Wonderland. How dare I be stepping out of the door while they have to hunt, cook, and eat in their PJs, and perhaps the world expects they will take a shower later? I tried very hard not to look at them, but I got goosebumps with my head down thinking about their search in my brain and heart.

Another month passed, everyday repeated like yesterday.

Nothing was interesting or exciting, and the news wasn't any help. After a temporary opening with limitations, we got back to lockdown with no access to theatre, shopping malls, travel, or gatherings. Schools were closed, too. The only accessible areas were parks and groceries. No dining or chatting with a friend in person. We all got back to our fourth dimension living in Wonderland without time or location dimensions. It didn't matter if it was three a.m. or six p.m. We could find someone in this surreal world to chat with, but somehow it wasn't encouraging. It was a time when we got up in the middle of the night, thought after a busy week, and spent time with family and friends after work, it was a good time; having a little space in the middle of the night with ourselves, drinking a glass of hot milk or hot chocolate, or even a glass of wine., but in Wonderland, getting up at three a.m. was another routine, like the day before, watching TV or reading a book or searching for a new way to get out of this box, and then going to sleep knowing there was no limitation for sleeping tomorrow morning. There was no work or real people waiting for us to eat breakfast with, and we won't be in a hurry to catch a train or get to work.

We were hoping to watch something with some signs of ending point to this situation and getting out of our box, and after we gave up on that, started to read news to see what was going on, and how this pandemic was taking over all the world, and even was closing the borders, but in Bermuda, we didn't have a strong receiver dish to let us know what is real news. Outside our underground life, everyone had forgotten us, and no matter what time it was, we were alone.

This chatting and talking in the virtual world got boring, and as we guessed, there wasn't anything we could discuss except those subjects that were in the news, it was lack of intimacy that we all were suffering from, but many of us prefer not to talk about it, and keep others away from judging us.

As much as every attendee in the virtual world was pretending to enjoy dancing, seminars, and gatherings online, we all knew it was just a hobby, like playing video games or listening to audiobooks, nothing more. Our roomies in virtual world was nothing like what we had in real world, where we could feel what they think, and in response, we were using our fifth sense to react. In that world, there was no need for that anymore; we could just turn our camera off or close our speaker, and like other times, just listen or watch like watching TV or listening to the radio.

It was a complete version of Wonderland. You could change your background and show you are in a jungle, or even in a galaxy. There wasn't any need for eye contact. Who are we supposed to look at? We were talking to groups of people and couldn't even see all of them on one screen. Slowly, we got tired of this new method that was created to make us busy and not think about where and when we got into this mess, so we changed those types of meeting to just watching movies and searching the internet alone. This way, there wasn't any need for sitting or be cut off by a random question from someone about a discussion you aren't interested in the first place.

This new world wasn't that bad for business, though. Everyone could sit in his home and do his work in whatever time or location he wanted. He could even take his laptop or cell into the washroom and work from there. It is called remote work. No one cares that this work is created in your living room or bedroom, plus, for emergencies in the country, many businesses are receiving a budget for themselves and their employees. We remembered how for those years in the real world, we were wishing for a few days' vacations, or even we had to go to work when we were sick. In this world, many people were making money and could provide food and tea on their tables and could watch rabbits sitting in their coffee cups regardless of how they spent their money.

It was a year after the pandemic and my birthday was coming. I thought, what now? What am I supposed to do this year for my birthday?

After a few days of thinking and searching, finally I decided to go for speed dating. This way, I could meet others who at least were brave enough to admit they were looking for a relationship in the real world. I registered and waited for my birthday. It was way better than those fake gatherings talking about nonsense. We knew why we were there and what we were looking for. At least this equation had some constants and a few variables. It wasn't a mystery. We were men and women looking for real feelings and it was only subject, no talking around or making stories or attacking those that were not on our sides, or making profiles based on who they think are your mates, or perhaps you had a relationship with. We knew probably it was another experiment, but it was fun after a long time living in Wonderland and talking to our smart devices.

At first didn't get anywhere but it made me try it again, unlike those boring gatherings. This one at least had another side interested, talking and chatting, even if there wasn't any connection. We spent a few weeks after my birthday in lockdown hoping this virus would be over soon. During these weeks, a new topic was in the news every day. Finally, vaccines were here and we could protect ourselves, many of us jumping up and down to celebrate and some running to call their families and friends on another side of the world to give them the good news that they will be alive and they are cheating on death.

In these confusing times, this new news changed our constant living situation. For a few days and weeks, many were happy and hopeful to get rid of this bubble, but very soon, it turned to another subject for everyday news and keeping us praying for our turns to be vaccinated. In this among, even we were not able to think about consequences because our options were either to live in a box and scared of dying, or take this vaccine and see what was going to happen. Some of us jumped on the opportunity to take the vaccines and pay for it no matter what, but some of us sat back and watched to see where this new subject for discussion was going. In either way it is a lose situation, but simply we believed in a win scenario to keep our hopes up for a better life.

We didn't know what it meant. Are we free of the disease now? Can we get back to our three dimensions, will be a protected underground world after being vaccinated in Wonderland? But either way, after a year and half hearing about this killing epidemic, it was a light at the end of the tunnel and it made us happy and grateful.

Since I didn't understand what this situation was all about, I waited to see what percentage of population around me was getting this vaccine. It was another competition like the first weeks of beginning pandemic that people were fighting for toilet paper and sanitizers. Now it was another war for who gets what and when scenario. Many scared people were looking around and asking everyone what they think, and if they should get it or not. Others were dying to get this vaccine and win this isolation competition, and among these, those who were rich didn't mind to pay thousands of dollars for black market, and this way, a medication which was imported or produced in the country for saving emergency situations became part of a black market, and accessing to it turned to a marathon.

First priority granted to the elderly population, which to me it was putting the elderly in the front line of experiments. No one knew being in priority group was good or bad, but it didn't matter either way. We were going to die from disease or vaccine. Therefore, the older generation proudly accepted be in the front row of receiving this magical mystery vaccine, and then this interest extended to others.

While we were waiting for our turns, we were praying this would be the end, and after that, someone would be opening the door to the outside world and set us free, but it did not happen. After the first priority group bravely took the vaccine, the younger noticed they still are alive accepted to be vaccinated too. It was another hot news, "No one can leave his house without mask regardless of vaccination," and we should remain in lockdown till everyone got vaccinated, and perhaps it was another sentence which we didn't hear but we know was there: "we'll see after that".

Survival groups got back to their caves and restrictions got tighter. No one understood why in Wonderland, in which we don't have anything except our food and rabbits, we were limited from visiting other parts of this Bermuda Triangle, but we still were very happy having food, being vaccinated, and alive, and the most important, our next generation would be alive and God's acts is deactivated.

During this long period of isolation, everyone tried to be thoughtful and creative. Some people in their basement started new businesses. Some started to find remote jobs and some others looked for who would do what scenario. Concerned authorities first kept alarming everyone and were exhausted of checking dead lists and registered hospitalization, but gradually they found out or admitted to themselves they knew it was not what it looked like.

This way they got creative too and started to make a solution. This process took a long time and many scared citizens and non-citizens got benefits of governmental financial assistance and they felt much better and forgot this killing disease existed and that they were in lockdown in their homes. In addition to foods and rabbits, now they have money without even going out of Wonderland. It wasn't that bad, after all, a few got crossed from the eligible list for receiving that assistance. I guess those were either part of sacrificed group in Bermuda or just simply they weren't good receivers for that assistance.

In my isolated box, I thought this financial assistance was like replacing a new organ in your body. Probably some people's blood tests would show they were not a good match, and if they receive it, perhaps their body wouldn't accept this treatment, or simply someone decided he should die and she should be saved, and then I realized those who are contributing money are very smart and think all aspects of this situation

We were waking up every day to watch news, read books and articles, and tried to be smarter, and like those who already are thinkers, find the best solution for ourselves. No matter that we are in our PJs, thinking about this disaster in the washroom, or while we were taking a shower. The most important point was we were smarter than before, because there was not any entertainment, outside gatherings, movie theaters, clubs, or even restaurant, so we had all day and night to ourselves to think and think and think, and this led us to overthinking and crushing down. When we could make a simple handcraft or could fix a small screw in our home, we knew we were way better than those who just sat on their couch and watched movies or listened to music. This way, we believed we were better and started to make fun of them, and anytime they stepped out of their box to get a coffee or go somewhere, with our glance and all types of sign languages, told them how dare they were not to stay home and make something or read a book. This was a new technique to make ourselves feel better while other groups thought the same.

In this process, most people changed from an active person to a disturbed person who was forced to do nothing, some from wasting time to a thinker, some from sad and disappointed to a very happy person who can work remotely and make money without any movement, and some even grew from their childhood to adulthood and they learned this is the way we should live. Our kids thought it was very exciting staying in your bed and making money with the digital world, and this way we all created more isolation, fears, and encouragement to stay in the comfort zone.

In Bermuda, we built our basic home and whatever we needed for a simple life, and if anyone tried to get more than the basic, we would attack him and put him outside our friend circles and thought, how could he? In this situation, we were after toilet paper and vaccinations, he thinks about sports or restaurants or more dangerous things like travel or shopping? In Bermuda, we do not need those things. We are not going outside and our family knows how we lie down on our couch and eat our burger and burp after. They know how we get angry with our kids or fight with our mates, so this way we, in every way, were moving backward, and living with rabbits did not bother us anymore, and we adopted living in Wonderland with the basics, with or without assistance.

In this underground living, those who already had family tried to stay away from any single, to make sure they owned their spouses and kids and no one could take them. This group became more aggressive and thought they had all the right in the world in Bermuda to keep their family safe and far from anyone who tried to make small talk, or without consideration, wanted to have a conversation, or worse than that, invited them to a party. Another group, who were living on their own, got more isolated and depressed knowing not only they did not have anyone on their side who could cry on their shoulders, but also they are not allowed to approach anyone inside the family, and their creative method failed with loneliness and fears or getting close to someone in the family.

Among this, no one understood that this basic living never could be improved the way we were trying too hard to keep our partners and relatives just for ourselves. On another side, those who thought they would die anyway, either by virus or side effects of the unknown vaccine, started to break their box and come out. This was a new beginning of a revolution. Those who for a long time had been trying to not be discovered and hid who they really were suddenly became themselves heroes. They admitted to having many potential abilities that they couldn't show by living on the Earth. They decided it was time to show everyone what they could do in the underground. It was like everyone was tearing his skin to come outside like a silkworm who turns into a butterfly, but it had the same problem as everything in the epidemic - that's why this equation wasn't right.

Some thought they had already turned into butterflies. Some thought, why should they remain silkworms when everyone else could fly? Some tried to compete with others to prove in basic life, there are better choices, and this list goes on and on.

At the beginning, everyone was so excited for these changes, and thought they would live in a new world with a new life. That's why, when borders were closed, no one even was bothered. Now we had our small Wonderland without any strangers, but gradually this ban extended to other parts of life like merchandise imports and exports, exchanging knowledge, or even a brain storm, and then like corrosion, moved in our souls and took our heart and feeling, and it was beginning of using the digital world for distancing and masking.

I tried to go out of my box again to discover around hoping to find a way to the outside world, stepped out of my door with my mask, walked out of the building main door, and surprisingly this time a few people were around. Radio and TV continuously announcing we all are in this together. For a moment, I thought, who else has been in this with me? It took a while for me to realize this sentence was related to buying toilet paper and food, not anything else. Then I took a deep breath and felt good I didn't miss anyone who apparently was in this with me and I didn't realize it.

While I was walking around, I noticed rabbits jumping up and down. I even followed them to see if they knew how we could get out, but they were brilliant and fast and in a blink of an eye, they disappeared. I guess they got back to underground. Since I couldn't find any door to outside and weather was very cold, my breathing had made my mask completely wet and cold. I gave up on finding any door out of isolation and went straight to the closest store to my home and bought tea and a new kettle to make sure I could drink tea no matter what.

Living in isolation was boring. At first, we were waking up early and were doing our routine to make sure we were not losing our good habits for the upcoming opening and getting back to normal life, but it was replaced by sadness and long waiting.

Before lockdown, we had options to pick what we wanted to do on the weekend or for our vacation, but in this new world, we were dying to go anywhere, no matter where it was. It would be shopping malls, museums, or even traveling around the city, just a way to get out of our dark cell, but there was no sign of hope. Before the pandemic, we thought travel was expensive, but after our borders were closed, we just wanted to travel, even to the smallest island in a hidden area which we were praying was different from Bermuda Island, but almost every country closed their territories to keep foods and medicines for their people. Besides, this way, they could control and supervise every move inside.

At first, it seemed a perfect plan. Everything was under control, but slowly, this isolation impacted on import and export, on jobs, schools, universities, and people changed to a new version of themselves; some very irritated of staying in their loneliness for long time, some thinking they had lost the important part of their lives, and some turned to the new champion of the digital world, and even society's vision changed, and living on a computer, tablet, and cell phone made most of us gain weight and do some stupid or crazy things which in normal life we never thought about it , like making a funny video.

In this waiting period, singles realized they missed those days that they were lucky and had a chance to like someone and get close to her or even ask her out, and families were exhausted of spending days and nights with their family. They used to get away from this repeating life now and then, but now they all were in a line up for getting a vaccine that apparently was the last hope for saving this planet.

Those who were very happy to see places never seen before were closing down their businesses, getting ready to jump on the first moving object travel to one of them regardless of how much they hated it. Younger generations who were more energetic and needed to release their inside power started to jump on every opportunity they got, from playing computer games, to attending international zoom conferences, chats, to online learning, but none of them were enough for making a healthy life. Most people were suffering from lack of affection that by warning about distancing and fear of getting the virus left them with no choice but to stay in the virtual world. Those who were living with their family and loved ones first were very happy, but gradually they started to argue, their differences that before were hidden or were invisible, showing up in the worst way.

Some groups decided to go outside and attend a rally to ask authorities when this situation was going to get better, hoping they would let them have a little more options, but this action made those who were scared to death and didn't believe in fighting with God's acts react. Then this situation not only wasn't any help, but also made a new excuse for more restrictions as they were carrying the killing virus, and now or in the future, they are who will be blamed.

However, this objection wasn't successful, but it was a new way for meeting others and feeling that someone somewhere thought like them, and there are others who want to get out and break this box, too. Besides, they could release their stacked energy before it exploded inside.

Time was flying on and while everyone was reacting in her own way, they all were accepting living with lower expectations, and it made them angry how their life had changed, and they took it out on others by attacking and questioning them why they changed their outfits or bravely laughed sometimes. It was the way how they got revenge on unknown diseases, by pointing at someone and feeling better.

Any time their friends and families asked them what was going on, their answer was loud and clear: "It is all about those who want to get out of Wonderland and ask for more options and opportunities, if they accept and adapt their lives like us, we do not have any disease and epidemic." With this answer, they taught how they could stop anyone asking for more, and just like historical events, a new internal fight started. Something they didn't know was when you are fighting with external power, it might be ended somehow, but inside fighting is way more dangerous than that, and it might get to long, long fights for generations and perhaps never ending.

One group always blames another group for what they lost and another side is angry for having different classes in society. In normal life, people are too busy with their life to think about this, except those who are part of a certain group, but in this isolation world, everyone became a new detective who wanted to know why her life had been changed without her request. They had all the time in the world to analyze what they did or did not. While most of us were busy trying to find a reason, a group of rabbits made a new theory: "If we make everyone just point out one person and direct them to find out if he is responsible for this epidemic or not, they get busy and do not look for a real reason".

It was a new revolution in Wonderland, and it was the moment I realized why rabbits are living in this underground life and why they always a few steps ahead of me and I never could catch them. With this discovery, I took a deep breath and felt relief and ran to my teapot and poured a cup of tea to drink. I thought, if I cannot live like a rabbit, it's better I drink my tea because no matter what, in Wonderland, we live with our teas and rabbits. While I was drinking my tea, I tried to laugh ,In my evil thought, I got to the point where I couldn't be as smart as a rabbit, but I could make them angry with my laugh because they have to release their power to make others focus on my attitude. It was one of the best cups of tea I ever drunk.

After every group successfully closed his territory our living areas turned to smaller islands, each group started to get whatever they could for their groups, from hunting animals, to collecting woods and leaves, for surviving longer times, and after a while, they felt their territory could expand and started to argue with neighbors about who is owner of what. Since this argument didn't get anywhere, they started to steal from each other when other groups were asleep. Everyone in each group had a skill or knowledge or a talent that could be added value to the group, but they gradually realized their knowing was not enough and other groups might know more, and it was the beginning of copying what this or that had. Sometimes, one or two of those units merged and made bigger, better groups that were more capable of fighting and improving. In this underground life, no one noticed how they were changing from a civilized modern community to fighters who are just after copying, but everyone was happy to have food and could drink tea and rabbits were around.

In this mess, those who were stepping on someone else right at first thought they were very smart like rabbits, but slowly their life changed and they were too busy even realize it. They kept playing with others' lives, lied and cheated and dug in others' personal lives, thought they could and would, but this scenario already had extended to all dimensions of everyone's life, and something they didn't predict was always there were others who were smarter, therefore, this cycle was never ending. Just like the food chain, animals feed from smaller animals, but they are hunted and could be eaten by bigger, more powerful animals, and this chain was from the first day of creation or evolution and no one knows when it will be ended. Living in Wonderland wasn't anything different, even worse than before. In this new life, everyone not only was after bigger territory, but also because access to basics was harder than before, they were ready to kill and eat smaller, even worse than the jungle.

The only difference was while we were living on Earth, we were usually busy in our life and possible families, and those cheaters and liars were limited, b ut in Bermuda, rabbits who apparently were smarter groups got involved with new theories for fighting and getting what others had and they didn't, and this way, power and energy were used in the dirtiest way. Since almost everyone was involved, they didn't understand they were losing to themselves, and their methods and this circle is never ending because no one tried to take a moment to think how those tricks that impact on someone else's life, will get back to them soon

They were happy and satisfied by stealing from others and attacking and accusing. This way, they felt better in this underground world and this corrosion extended in every single part of life, like how water flows in a foundation, but in other parts of the structure, wasn't anything visible. That's why they were celebrating their victory and thought they were winners, and apparently any other groups except rabbits were losers, but no one understood the foundation of this society and life is going down every day, slowly and dangerously.

After a while, when those small groups thought they were done with building their basic homes and were safe with their friends and family, was time they watch over other units and groups, to see if they have something they do not t and based on historical data, they believed successful people are those who take from every unit.

Before they had everything they wanted and never had thought about their neighbors belongings, but in Wonderland, sitting on the food table and living in the virtual world made them realize they were not as good as they thought, and it was the beginning of stealing and copying from each other. This wave moved to relationships, emotions, and feelings, and they gave the right to themselves to take over others' families, friends, hobbies, food, and at any opportunity they got, attacked their neighbors and anyone they could take something from, and just like millions of years ago, after they killed men, they took women and kids as slaves made them work and built a life they had seen other units have.

At first, it was just like a game or just a childish jealousy, but it extended to the fourth dimension. We already had lost our three dimensions of our life, and damaging this fourth dimension and taking over our virtual world that was the only window to the outside was a disaster. In this situation those who could get weapons, more money, and get to Wonderland earlier took over other units, and by merging with other groups, made their territories bigger and bigger. That way, after a while, no one could exist to fight against them.

Our men were out of pictures and our kids brainwashed to adopt this new basic life, and if they wanted to survive, they should be part of bigger units. Most women, especially those who their time for having babies had passed, and were not able to bring new kids for bigger groups, were considered as slaves who should work and obey. Younger women were new birth machines for creating a new generation in the underground world, powerful units expanding their generation and they needed a healthier and stronger race for their birth machine, and this way, many survivors were eliminated under tremendous pressure, or simply pushed to invisible groups. Bigger units were counting on taller, stronger, healthier generations and hoping they could take over everything in Bermuda. On other side, those who were to be held at a certain level either accepted their situation without questioning, or were labeled as rebellious, and with this method some units got smaller and smaller and disappeared. After a long time living in Bermuda, when units realized there was no way they could get out of this life, they started to be scared either of losing their power and whatever they had stolen, copied, or taken from other units, or for being eliminated and pushed to invisible groups, and it was the moment they pulled a fence around their units and tried to have shift days and nights, but it wasn't any help because either way, we all had fallen in that hole a long time ago, and if we had realized it instead of trying to take over other units, we could have worked together to find a way to the outside world, but it was too late.

This ignorance and negligence that was called God's acts and apparently had absolutely no solution made all of us stuck in this new living style, which many bigger groups thought was the best life they could have after taking whatever they didn't have from others and becoming a big power, but this method already had moved to the basics of our life. Time was flying on and those birth women were getting older and the next generation had learned for having anything simply can attack others and take or copy it, and men, if they were not in a fight, became new Gods in their unit who no one could say anything against their words, Older men who couldn't go to war or produce kids had the same situation as women. Either they were eliminated, or for survival, turned to a bully and gradually got closer to rabbits that were sitting and watching women and kids, drinking teas, and making sure they had food and tea cups.

In this isolated world, groups did not try to think better or be creative, instead just spying on other groups to see what they do, eat, how they work, and what they have or what is their plan, and this way, they got busy and were happy working and spending their time on something without knowing those jobs and work they created is wasting their life and harassing others, but since their territories were fenced, they couldn't know if other groups knew about their plan and work, or if it was a trick that made them get busy and forget they are living in an underground world with basics.

We were getting used to what we had and how we used others for our profits. We even used our kids and pets for following and spying on other groups, and thought we were teaching them how to survive, but in reality, we were teaching them nothing has more value than taking over other life, money, jobs, and overall their world.

We were turning to a close-minded every day, slowly, that we couldn't realize how we were eliminating some races, nationalities, ages, genders. Among this, we had learned that if someone says something or tries to warn us, blame her for our disaster, and perhaps cooperating with God that all our trouble was because of him. We were a better group if we had more money, kids, and horsepower, and others were easy targets to be labeled and kicked out of our world.

After almost one and half years, and finding how other fenced their territories with made vaccines, our hopeless situation changed to how and when we could get it.

I even decided to get vaccinated since it seemed was only

way out after trying night and day, finally I got an appointment and took a deep breath. It was a huge success in Bermuda. . After I booked my appointment, I tried to go out of my box again to see what was happening, if not out of our fenced world, at least inside. I stepped out of the door, nothing was changed, everyone was wearing a mask, some even two layers of masks, like they wanted to make sure this killing virus, if it could pass the first mask, will be stopped with the second layer. The street was dead, stores all closed except some grocery stores and drugstores. When we were passing we tried not to look at each other, thinking, what if this disease is carried by looking at each other. We had heard in the news all the time, do not touch your face and eyes, keep your mouth shut, and have distance with anyone around you. Then we thought, what if health systems forgot to tell us don't look at each other, or do not call or chat. Who knows, it might pass through your computer and cell phone. Then I thought, isn't that the reason in the virtual world some people had been kicked out of rooms? Or some other groups just accepted locals, not internationals?

After a long time, for the first time, I was very happy that I am alone and part of a smaller group because even when you live with bigger groups, or with your families and partners, you are not supposed to touch each other and their territory's air is full of virus, no matter how many layer masks they are wearing, and it made me happy like a kid who is getting revenge on the adults who sent her to detention.

After a long period of time, I had gained lots of weight like everyone else. We were sitting on the couch, eating and sleeping and sometimes following rabbits, nothing more. Walking with extra weight was difficult, but I got to the bus station, anyway. When I saw the bus was coming, it was like a spaceship coming to save me from the Earth. It stopped in front of me. I jumped on but it wasn't better than our underground life. The bus was empty and including me, around three brave people were there, with a pager continuously announcing to not get on the bus except with a mask, and in front of the bus was a huge sign lighting "just emergency travel". While I was sitting on the bus I was looking at the street, in which barely a few people were walking, but surprisingly the street were full of cars, and inside them mostly without masks. Does it mean inside cars the virus can't live, and inside the bus they are everywhere? Those who were scared to die from this deadly virus were looking at me and two other passengers like we are criminals who escaped from a jail, but no one even though why those cars were on the street. It was a warning that even police could stop you and ask why you were on the street or far from home, but I didn't see anyone stop or ask those cars where they were coming from or going. I even had noticed during Halloween and Christmas, there was a specific celebration for those who had cars, and without going out of their car, could watch decorations and enjoy, but the three of us on the bus were brave criminals who perhaps were going to do some grocery shopping to make sure our long table in Wonderland will have something on.

After I got off the bus, I noticed even walking on the street for smaller, weaker groups was considered a crime, and in front of the grocery store was a long line which, while I was walking to the line, some cars stopped and dropped off some passengers to make sure they got to the store before us. Then I realized why this line was not moving. For some unknown reason, I wanted to laugh, but that was another reason I was a criminal, laughing under my mask, that definitely had a big penalty and punishment. That's why I pulled my hat to my face and tightened my mask to prevent more criminal acts.

After this brave act, I got back home and sat on my couch to do some research. I was wondering why Wonderland is a kid's story and how we got in, since I wasn't a rabbit. For doing this research, I spent too much thinking. After several days and nights, thinking finally like an inventor who invented or discovered something, I got it. The reason we are all stuck here, and kids are happy and relaxed in Wonderland, is because they still don't know how to lie. We didn't have time to teach them lie to make adults happy. That's why they live in Wonderland happily ever after, and I am sure all parents are very proud to see their kids are honest and tell the truth, except that moment they tell the truth about them, about their mistakes, about what we did and what we shouldn't do, and how we cover our lies and mistakes which is not fair. At this moment, adults get mad and yell at their kids to stop following rabbits. Don't take tea cups, stay quiet, don't move, and in case, they do not listen to them who are smarter and stronger and in control. They use their strong arms and power to sit them in a limited place, or make them stand on one foot and raise their hands; or worse than that, if kids do not listen to them, or none of them could shut them up, then adults put pepper in their mouth or make them bite their tongue, and this way, teach them they just can tell the truth if it is in their benefit. If not, they will be punished and everything will be taken from them till they learn when they are allowed to tell the truth.

This discovery was the best part of living in the underground. Now I know why rabbits have longer teeth: for biting those who live in smaller and weaker groups, or didn't learn when they should talk about the truth. Then I tried to think about Alice; she was as confused as me, not understanding how we fell down in the hole and why everything is surreal here. I ran to my teapot to pour a cup of tea, but as soon as I tried to drink, my tongue and teeth hurt.

In this critical situation, something that didn't make sense was how animals behaved. I was taught when any of God's acts are happening, animals are the first group to feel it and run to protected areas. But in this epidemic, dogs and cats were trying to approach humans while they wore masks. For some reason, my balcony was full of birds, way more than before, and some birds that usually do not fly in big cities were in the sky. Then this question came to my head: "Animals didn't feel any danger? Does it mean this epidemic is not as bad as we think? How come I feel threatened, but not animals?" After spending three times more than rabbits thinking, finally I gave up and couldn't realize what was going on.

I got back to our virtual world to see what was going on there. As soon as I opened my computer, I noticed I was bombarded with zoom call conferences, virtual webinars, and online speeches and courses, and many of them were offered even for free. In my shocking mood, I thought, is that because before this epidemic, many organizations didn't know how to use this world, or they are so excited to see how they can sit with their families and invite others to listen to their speeches and conferences? Either way, it was good and bad news. Good news it could have shortened the time for getting jobs done, and using technology was a big jump from the nineteenth century to the new world. Bad news, it didn't matter if you could do a week or a month's work in five minutes; still you should sit at your table till the estimated duration to be ended. Considering this killing disease and epidemic, it was crazy for you to speed your work up. What would others think about us? Are we healthy and happy and can do our work faster with better quality? Then what happens after this epidemic is over? Should we work more productively and get paid less? For these reasons, we sit on the couch and postpone our meetings, or sometimes just cancel them, but we did not stop sending all types of online advertising and announcements about what we were doing or planned to do in this critical situation.

This up and down for opening and closing businesses and entertainments and social gatherings made people jump out of their skin anytime restrictions were loosened up, and be scared and depressed when it came back to the previous situation. One day, I, like millions of others, heard parks and sports courts were opened. I walked to the park with my mask and of course two meters away from everyone. It was one of those days where restrictions partially lifted. Parks were full of people and one of the biggest achievements for those who were sitting in the park or playing in the basketball and tennis courts after a long time in lockdown. While I was passing them with distance, I was sure I had read in Bermuda and lost islands stories about how when people's lives are limited, and many restrictions are in place, a little freedom is like they are coming back to life from death. But this was a live demonstration of what I had read before. Kids who usually prefer to sit beside their parents and ask for snacks now suddenly jumping in sports courts and playgrounds. Adults either were sitting on grass having a picnic or walking proudly like they were survivors of this epidemic and could get to this point and deserve this freedom.

After a few weeks, again most areas went into lockdown, and when I stepped out of my building to walk in the park, not even one person was around. I know these types of approaches are part of underground living. This way, either you are waiting for just a little freedom, or are using everything after a small lifting of restrictions. In this situation, I didn't understand how we got from last year getting ready for celebrating Christmas to this year's summer. Last time I was out, it was freezing cold and I had to cover my face, head and body with warm clothes, hats and scarves, but this time, after months of lockdown, when I stepped out, I was boiling in my light rain jacket. Then I thought how long I was in this situation. I noticed besides gaining weight, I slept more, and it was not just me. When I was out of home and looked at others faces, it was clear they just woke up, or long hours staying in their homes and on the food tables made them sleepy. Their eyes were tired and their faces out of masks were swollen. Then I remembered we are not allowed to wear makeup, change our clothes, or even smile. If anyone does this, it means she does not feel fear of this epidemic and even could be the reason of it. The good part was they couldn't see your lips behind your mask if you smiled, but you had to be careful to not show your smile in your eyes because they might order you to wear patches on your eyes like pirates to make leveling among those who try to live and those for whom their living is dependent on others.

As we guessed, a few people became candidates for being leaders. That's why they came out of their territories slowly and asked other leaders to find a way out of the underground. We searched every spot in this area and suddenly we noticed a narrow light was showing up in a corner. We lined up to get to this light and take a breath while a fresh air was coming through this hole. We were wondering if we could go up on the ground, but now we just had to stay in line and take advantage of a little fresh air. I don't know if it was a miracle of the New Year, or waiting a long time in Wonderland, but whatever it was made us search for a new way to know if there was any life in another island, like those time astronauts who were looking for a place beside Earth to find life on another planet, but this time was very different. We already had sunk into basics, and there wasn't any ambition for finding life or alliance in the galaxy. We were happy with finding a light or seeing if someone was living like us on another island. Last time we used all our bravery to get out of our door; this time was a big step to see who still was living, and how in this disaster, those volunteers decided to find a bigger hole in the corner and discover what was happening outside, and we patiently got back to our small territories and waited. After the waiting time was over, we heard some good news: there are others who live like us. In their territories and inside their fenced land, but no one knew what they did to fight with this unknown disease and what their plan for getting out was.

Either it was changing weather from cold and cloudy to sunny and warm, or it was the magic of discovery that made us feel better. On one of those days, I stepped out and surprisingly noticed more people were out. Some of them looked very sad to see how their life changed from up level living to basic. Some were jubilant they could be on the same level with those who never thought they could live like them. Some were excited they were alive, and some were looking for better options. No matter what we were thinking or feeling, we were in a critical situation that apparently God had created to probably test us, or perhaps punish us. We didn't know why we were in this situation, but it was good to see everyone was on the same boat and no one could escape from God's acts.

While we were waiting for our vaccination turn, we didn't stop living in the virtual world and tried to get as much information as we could about how they feel, what they do, and what is their status. This way, we thought we were living our life, but the reality was we got busy with searching, listening, and talking about this unknown situation. We knew how most of us reacted to the vaccine when it started, but again, it was either living under masks forever or getting the vaccine and getting out of that corner light. After months thinking and planning and seeing how brave front lines were getting vaccines, we believed we could block God's acts. It was a moment of excitement as we jumped out of our skins and lined up for receiving the antivirus and prayed the next step is getting out of our fences and probably meeting a human from another isolated planet, and it was one of the most critical tasks in the epidemic journey.

It was a group discussion everywhere about what we should do about this light and when time is and who should get out first. Finally, a group of those who usually in Bermuda were volunteers got together and started to follow this light and slowly got out, while others were in line and waiting to see what was going to happen to them. The outside situation was a bit different with underground living. It was air, light, and hopes. When this group got to the ground, they noticed other groups from other islands were there, and for the first time after a long time, they could talk face to face. Of course, under masks, this movement was like walking on the moon for the first time, or discovering Mars with a bit of difference. That time success was worth celebrating and failure just had financial loss or perhaps a few fatalities, but this time it was fighting with unknown factors that no one knew where they came from, plus, different groups had different ideas about the sources. Either way, it was a dangerous risk.

Living in the dark for long time led us to think groups on the ground couldn't see clearly, and this was making the situation worse. The first step to solving any problem is to know what it reason and to have a clear picture of the situation, but when you cannot see what is going on, and fear is involved, anyone could be the source, and perhaps that's why we wore masks in the first place.

While those groups were discussing and negotiating about who got what, we were in the underground trying to survive with jealous neighbors and limited possibility in Bermuda, but still we could drink tea and run after rabbits, and they were very smart moves from those behinds masks for encouraging us to follow rabbits. This way, we thought we were doing something and were too busy to think when or how we fell in that hole.

This lifting restrictions and going back to lockdown happened several times, and it was another sign of how we all somehow melted into the virtual world, like computers, cell phones, or other digital devices which, no matter how many antiviruses you downloaded, still suddenly your system was shutting down with viruses, and after you kill and clean it, it happens over and over, either with a new virus or because when a virus gets in your system, it can hide somewhere and move to other places. Living in the epidemic was the same situation. With all types of cleaning and protections, the virus was eliminated, but it came back again.

I thought we probably should take the same action we take with our computer after a virus had already moved deep in our system and we cannot do anything about it, and no new antivirus, nor restarting and shutting down, was working. We usually, in this situation, reset our system in factory set-up. Suddenly, it was horrifying: what does it mean if we want to reset our world to factory set-up?

A few times we observed what was happening after lifting restrictions and going back to lockdown, and this new antivirus was a new hope, but what we didn't realize was we already had reset our lives to basic and were very happy we were protected and the virus was not inside our groups. Exactly like when you are suspicious of any computer software virus in your system, you try to eliminate them or remove and install your programs again. We were doing the same; first we started to investigate or assume this killing virus was from this or that, and then tried to eliminate it and reinstall some of the eliminated stores, products, lifestyles, and even people, but it wasn't enough. Then we realized the virus still exists. Therefore, we decided to fence around our territories to make sure the virus was not inside, but no matter what we were doing, this disease was already in our system, and after any celebration, it was another stay home order.

This back and forth was eating our efforts and energy and had costs. After the antivirus was discovered and somehow got inside, we install them all over our world to control this virus. No one knew where the virus was hiding and how much damage was created, but we were busy with living in chat rooms and conference meetings and had little time to think about how and when we reset our life to the factory set-up.

However, we had the antivirus, fenced our home and controlled every movement, but what was killing us was this suspicion about everyone and everything. This unknown phenomenon had made us blame anyone who was doing what we didn't, and accuse others for falling in Wonderland, and it was a serious situation on top of what we were facing because of the virus.

We all were sitting in our small world to watch who does what, to make sure if something happens now and then, we have a person to blame and point at him for what we are going through. In this situation, those who hadn't this strong suspicious feeling were the best target. We were asking ourselves, how come they are not blaming and not accusing? It must be something behind this calmness, and this way we were in a loop, investigating, finding something, blaming, celebrating, finding is not the reason, being worried and sorry, investigating something else, finding a new reason and on and on and on, and time was flying on and we all were very busy.

Since we gave this right to ourselves to find something or someone to blame for what they do, we tried not to do anything to lead others to blame us. This shadow spread on all over our life and pulled us to live like in cave-living times to make sure we were not losing this right to blame others, and we lived in the underground world for a long, long time to make sure we were not getting sick with the virus.

The weather was getting warmer, but unlike those days we were living free of accusations, fears, and pointing to someone else or spending time going to the swimming pool, eating something on the patio, celebrating sport events in bars or stadiums, or going for a family picnic. We celebrated our taking the vaccine and having a chance to walk on the street without a mask, and it was the best spring summer we had after a while.

While we all were waiting for outside leaders to make a decision, I took another brave step out of my comfort zone and went out of my building. Somehow the way was darker than before. I was trying to double check our narrow light outside to make sure there was still a way out of this disaster. On my way to that corner light, I reviewed the similarity of our Wonderland to the digital world, and suddenly I got goosebumps after realizing when my computer had a virus, I could reinstall software, but if it had damaged my hard disk, there was no way I could reuse it, and my thoughts went to the hard part of our world and I noticed our planes, trains, buses and cars were not running. We could reproduce merchandise, reopen stores, or rebuild some broken chains, but hard parts might never get back to the way before the pandemic. With these thoughts, I ran to the narrow light and lined up to make sure that before our hard disk is burned and all systems shutdown, we could get out of Bermuda, and prayed someone or some group could save us or at least know we exist. In the line-up, underground electricity started to blink and it was a sign that God's acts are getting seriously dangerous. For a moment, I wished I could see some rabbits around to know that besides us, they are trapped in this world too, but I guess they felt it before me and hide somewhere. In disappointment and fear, I wished I could at least drink my tea, the only thing still available, and no matter if software or hardware are impacted, I can drink it, but even that one wasn't possible. I looked behind to see if anyone was standing in the row with a cup of coffee or tea and then checked my front rows, but they all were standing at a distance to make sure could blame someone else for not having tea or coffee later, and as soon as my eyes caught their eyes, they pretended to be very busy with something which we both knew did not exist, and we all waited and waited for the unknown results of this epidemic.

During this up and down, a group didn't consider who was in lockdown with them. It didn't matter if their neighbors were sick, had a headache, or simply liked to live in her quiet world. They selfishly, by jumping and doing something, had created an impossible situation for others and were trying very hard to show others are active and doing sports or exercise. Interestingly, they were very proud of what they were doing, like they needed to prove no matter what, they were fit and sporty. This attitude extended to limited walks out in the park and sports courts. The way these groups were looking at others; like they deserved all freedom and others should sit on their table in their territories and eat food and drink tea with rabbits, but something they missed were those who had to spend more time than necessary in the virtual world or on their tables, were gradually were discovering a new version of the new world and perhaps could use it later, no matter if they were fit or not. Regardless of who belongs to which group, it was an inside war and each group took their anger and anxiety, the result of a long period living in lockdown, out on another group.

Discussion on the ground was in progress and this narrow hole was getting bigger and bigger and we were trying hard to believe we successfully would pass God's test for staying in our home for more than one and half years, which before, we even couldn't think about, especially for those who are fit.

This adopted underground world has changed many of us. Living in our PJs and using our computers in washrooms and our cell phones in the middle of the night in our bedroom had created a new world which we didn't know was good or bad. What we knew was we had been forced to live this way and it was a solution rabbits had found, and some ordinary people like me never could understand.

In this situation, what I knew was I needed to breathe and find a way to get out to the ground, and if in my past life I never thought I should discover other sides of borders, now I was dying to get out of my fenced world. In the meanwhile, time flies on, and no one knows what is next. Should we use our remaining time to go somewhere? Does someone know we are alive here? I was tired of wearing a mask and sitting on the table with rabbits who barely could keep up with their IQ. I needed a group of people like me to laugh, talk, cry, get happy and upset, dress up or stay in their PJs, go for a ten minute walk or sit in a coffee shop for long duration just because we don't want to stay home alone, or dance and jump to make themselves forget about their problems, none of which were possible in this new adopted world.

It takes months for us to successfully book an appointment to receive a vaccine. On one side, we were too busy to search and book an appointment to realize months passed without doing anything useful, but on the bright side we could get the antivirus and perhaps get out of Bermuda before the island disappeared.

I will never forget the day I was going to get my vaccine was like a remembrance day, the day survivors were coming back from war. I stepped out of my apartment to get to my appointment and after fifteen minutes, I was protected from viruses and God's acts. After almost eighteen months, I came out of my appointment thinking, now everything changes and we get back to our normal life, or someone comes and take us out of the underground, but surprisingly, nothing changed. I waited for weeks and examined those places we usually used to go before the epidemic but no, the outside world was dead and people got used to living the way they were living in the last eighteen months. I tried to be positive and gave time to the underground life to get better, or at least improve, but nothing happened. We were wearing masks and restrictions were in place and we got back to our virtual world.

I thought, I might be missing something, and that's why I started to listen to news again. They were talking about this antivirus proudly and how not only they help everyone with this vaccine, but also are helping other fenced worlds. For some reason, I couldn't understand now that we were vaccinated, why we couldn't get back to our old lifestyles.

In this continuous advertising about vaccines over and over, we were informed the first dose wasn't enough and the main reason we were not out of Wonderland was because of that. Okay, now I feel better; it means after the second dose, we are free to live without getting blamed, being a target of jealousy, we will stop digging in others' lives and live in a world without borders? I can wait another three to four months for the next vaccine. Then I calculated with this extra waiting how long I had been living in Bermuda, and suddenly I freaked out when realized I was getting older and taking one step closer to death with every extra waiting time, but alive or dead, we were living in Wonderland anyway, and nothing was real. There is no need to be scared; it is a virtual world, and perhaps we can reboot the world and get back to life after death. We are not living in the real world. I took a deep breath wore my mask and bravely I walked for ten minutes in the park close to my building and got back to my apartment, ate on long tables, and watched rabbits jumping up and down and chewing anything around. I thought, even rabbits don't understand what this is. Probably that's why they left these unknown risks category and God's acts theory behind. With those scary thoughts I ran to my teapot and poured another cup of tea to know at least I am still that real to feel hot tea in my mouth, and then sat on my couch and like Alice, got back to our new Wonderland after vaccination.

That way every day. In the morning, I was getting up to take a shower and accept all blame from the world for being clean and changing my PJs, or perhaps brushing my hair and sitting on my coach to see when this outside discussion was getting somewhere. In this process, I was annoyed to notice how others pointed at anyone cleaned up to make themselves feel good. Interestingly, they were the same group who had been doing this for long time, but I guess I was too busy to pay attention, and now for drinking too much tea, I could see them through my drunk eyes of tea.

After getting the first dose of vaccine, people still preferred to stay home, stores and offices were closed, and you couldn't realize who was behind those masks. I thought I would give it another few weeks and then check it again. In the meanwhile, I was following news to see what new good news was, but all I was hearing was how the antivirus is here and people should get it as soon as possible. If it wasn't very good news, at least it wasn't bad news, either. It means we should wait a bit longer. This longer waiting period hit me badly. When we are talking about a little bit, what does it mean? Little compared to big or large is little, but what is their definition? Is a decade big or little? How about a month? How much times do I have to wait a little bit more?

Anyway, I waited more this virtual world and having meetings with my monitor wasn't attractive any more. Either it was because I was tired of waiting, or those who were hiding behind this digital world would make it hard to be interested. It might be because I needed to meet and talk to other humans face to face, for not forgetting I am not a robot. Suddenly I realized for a period of lockdown, I was talking to Alexa and Bixby. However, inside my heart it was some type of fear, but I thought at least I still can talk and did not forget how to speak due to not talking to anyone for a long, long time.

After months I decided to get out and see what has been changed. Hoping I would see a lot more than before, I stepped out. The street was still dead. A few people were walking, coffee shops and restaurants still closed, and grocery stores were opened with limited capacity. I wasn't following school news since I do not have kids, but I thought how long parents kept their kids inside and if this lockdown lifted, how they could back to their normal life? At this moment, I suddenly felt very good that I don't have kids in school. Dealing with them before and after couldn't be easy, and this epidemic for sure would impact on their personality, and psychologically it will have consequences.

Our next generation won't let their kids go outside to play, and if they complain, they will tell them how they were stuck at their home for years without school or friends, and with limited access to their needs. Those were scary thoughts, but on bright side, I won't be alive to see that, since still I am in the waiting time frame and who knows when this little bit will be finished.

Like the last one and half years, I did my grocery shopping, watched my TV, ate, slept, and sometimes had meeting virtually and of course drank tea. It seemed even rabbits were tired. They couldn't jump up and down any more. For some strange reason, it looked like they were less than before. Did it mean they had to keep distance from other rabbits and couldn't get in any relationships, or their relationships were broken because of this unknown virus, and that's why they are less than before? During this long waiting period, anytime I was going outside, I was seeing rabbits were there and it made me happy to know some other live creatures were around, but they were gradually disappearing. Before, when I was sitting on my couch, I could see rabbits in my teacup, but not any more. Did it mean we were not living in Wonderland any more? When were we kicked out of Wonderland? With those thoughts, I ran to the narrow light to see what was happening during those months after my first vaccination. Still it was a long line in front of that hole and I guess we all were waiting to hear some news from outside the underground, and our messengers to outside would tell us they rebooted our world and we could get back to normal. However, the hole was bigger and we could hear some discussion from outside, but this long line and anyone who was waiting for some rescue crew or a ship from the ocean to take them out of Bermuda looked tired and older and their eyes didn't have any flame for living. It was like we all got back from death.

I passed all the long line and jumped to the front row and tried to climb, but it was rocky and I injured myself. I got back down and looked at the long line to see if anyone, anyone was interested to climb with me, but they all stole their looks and pretended they couldn't see or hear me. Then I felt I really wanted to see rabbits, but they were not around, either. We had lost Wonderland too, and this time, we were really close to be disappeared in Bermuda.

For some reason, I didn't want to go back to my couch without getting results. Therefore, I started to scream hoping someone could hear us, but except the echo of my voice, nothing came back. I got back home and turned on the TV, listening to the news, praying something good would happen or someone would tell something, but it was like a broken record, the same news over and over and over.

Days after days, and months after months passed. There wasn't any new news about this pandemic, but either people were tired or they didn't want to pick between being sick or living in isolation. Around six months, after producing the vaccine, I see some movement around. While I was walking in the park, I noticed unlike before all the sports courts were opened, and suddenly everyone was interested in cycling, basketball, tennis, and other sports courts were busy. While I was passing, I thought, are they really enjoying sports, or just like me, they want to do something to make sure they are still alive? Either way, it was good to see some people were coming out and at least trying to break the fear.

This getting vaccinated was everyday news and authorities were encouraging everyone to get their first dose, and the first row who already had gotten their first dose could get the second one. Wow, we thought we'd be free in a few months. Priority groups run for the second dose and after a while accelerated appointments were permitted. I was wondering how everyone reacts after getting vaccinated. While I was on the bus to do grocery shopping, I tried to look around. Except for those who have cars, a few people were on the bus or in stations. Most stores were still closed, some businesses in fear, and disappointment had added a space in front of their stores for accepting customers outside. For some reason, they thought outside, the virus is not as active as inside, or we are told that. Some revolutionaries were outside without masks. Either they were trying to be very brave or just simply tired of not breathing. Streets were still empty and sad. I got off the bus at my destination. For a minute, I didn't recognize this route I used to travel for the last six years almost twice in the week. It was quiet and barley any pedestrians were passing, but inside, the store was crowded. This made me believe I was right; except our tea and food, we have nothing else to make us alive, and who knows, we might lose buying food in the future because of not working or closed businesses. At this moment, I pushed my card to the isles and bought everything, as much as I could. It was what I had in that moment without limitation or restriction. Interestingly, while I was waiting in line to self-check, I noticed most of the customer's carts were full of food and, of course, toilet paper, which apparently was the main necessary product for living in a pandemic.

Since I did not have a car, I called a Lyft for getting home, and it takes hours to sanitize and sterilize everything. I never heard from the news about washing or sanitizing everything you buy, but assumed it was a good way to protect inside my home from viruses.

Following my first speed dating on my birthday, I gave it another shot to see how this virtual world works. Most of the assigned dates were with those we already met on our first date and wasn't any connection. A few were new, and finally I made a date to meet someone. Our meet up was weird and strange, just like he was in his teen age and played kid games. It was very clear he is on mission to play a game that online dating is not working, deep down, I could see he was a nice guy, but I couldn't understand why he was playing. Is this epidemic situation making people act like a kid? Overall, it was an interesting and bizarre date. It made me want to let all guys like him, if they want to play games, live in their childish world instead of having a new friend or relationship, especially in this time of isolation.

I don't know if it was lack of affection or living a long time in isolation that led men and women behave strangely. in return to a simple approach like saying hi to someone or asking a question or simply smiling at them, either you told them you are ready to get married or at least sleep with them, and if not those, you must want something from them, probably money or a job, or you are escaping from a mystery crime and need to hide. This weird behavior was everywhere the way I even couldn't ask a person for directions or say hi, just because they thought if I am not asking to sleep with them, probably I met them in my childhood or my exes look like them. In those situations, I couldn't keep myself from laughing and thought we really fell down in that hole a long time ago and these people forgot in the civil world we say hi and how are you to each other, go on normal dates, like or hate someone, or simply just don't want them to be part of our living circle. This epidemic would make all of us notice how far, far away from the civil, advanced world we live. It was another hitting time to my head that I realized, no, I don't want to live with these people who act in this hole. I want to climb and go outside, meet normal people who do not react to your hi or look at you as the worst enemy ever. That's why I ran to the narrow light, looked up, and listened carefully to see if anyone outside was trying to take us out of this isolated, scary, uncivilized world.

This cave living and fencing had caused most isolated people to be curious about how another person live, what she eats, where she goes and what she says, and even line was crossed and personal life and personal documents was attacked. They were tired and disappointed of not having a normal life, and if before they couldn't improve because of what situation they had created and were responsible, today they even couldn't try because of this killing virus. Therefore, their only hobby became spying on their neighbors, friends, or even their families. It was like they all were looking for something to cover this situation, and it was nothing better than following and spying on someone else and labeling her as this and that. This way not only they were busy in their caving life, but also they had a new subject to discuss in their small isolated fenced area. I observed for almost the length of the epidemic to see what it was all about, this curiosity, spying and labeling, and the only thing I got was perhaps it makes them feel they are doing something, or in their imagination, they need to be liked. Or simply was their only hobby in that moment

I saw they were looking for something to hang in there, and since they just have tea and toilet paper, and live in a virtual world in which anyone can lead them to any path they want, the only thing left for them was this imagination and accusation. This way, they feel better and feel alive and it was another sign that we fell down in the hole a long, long time ago.

A few months later, many businesses reopened and people were free to catch a movie, go shopping, or even dine in, but surprisingly, most of us got used to this isolation and comfort zone. We thought, why should we bother ourselves when we can sit in our PJs and even eat our lunch or dinner without limitation or time restriction, rather than getting out of our home for seeing someone in person. For this reason, outside was still very empty like the population was dead a long time ago. The bus station which usually was very crowded looked quiet, but strangely those who had a car were driving everywhere without wearing masks, and looked like they were enjoying life from the comfort of their car through driving to the drive through cinema, food pick-up, and celebrating occasions, while our share was sitting in our house and watching them how having fun without getting contaminated with the virus. Any time I was in the bus station, I was asking myself, why am I not driving in this underground world while we are stuck here? Any way and every time, I figured out my share was standing in the bus station and walking during the pandemic to be tested if I can get this disease, or it is safe for others to come out, and this way, I was satisfied with myself for this bravery which had been given to me, and I was celebrating this given mission by drinking more tea and running after rabbits.

I don't know if it was this disease or sitting a long time in my apartment that made me be slower than before, and it wasn't just me. While I was walking, I looked at other people. It was like watching a movie in slow motion; we all were talking, walking, even thinking slowly, and that's why rabbits were the winners of this Bermuda living. Every day I was looking myself in the mirror and noticing I was gaining weight, and there was no way of escaping from this underground. Even after, when stage three of reopening was in place, reduced hours, the long line in front of every store, washing your hands hundreds of times for entering every store, health checks and registration before taking off for any destination, and even measuring your temperature and asking you the same health questions over and over led us to prefer to stay home rather than go out. We couldn't use our inside gym, swimming pools, or even the lobby. The only place we were allowed to live was inside our fencing world and our hobby had turned to spying on those who were going out even for a minute.

This waiting time was killing many of us, but many others accepted this living style and your resistance was a sign of disobedience, and for some reason, they think it is against them, and in this confusion, on top of limited living and restrictions, a new inside war was in progress, and no matter who was doing what, another group was questioning them. With this new hobby, spying, comparing, threatening and taking our anger on anyone whose life style was different, we couldn't realize time was flying on and we were in isolation almost for two years and no one knows how long more. In this messed up underground world, still there was a narrow light from outside and I was running to that light every day to look for new hope and updates. It was a discussion, and I could hear conversations from outside. Sounds like leaders were trying, but time was passing very fast and many of us, including leaders, already gave up on living normally, and even thought there was not any other living style except what we already accepted.

The good news was that this narrow crack was expanding slowly, following serious action from the second dose of the vaccination for everyone regardless of who is priority, which as we heard, was the end of this pandemic, and we could go out and perhaps get out from Bermuda, before this one disappeared like our Wonderland. This news was everywhere, no matter what time of day or night, or if it was pacific or Eastern Time, or time was calculated based on the Greenwich clock. It was first news from all communication channels everywhere in the world. Then I thought, is that why it didn't matter we started our new year with two days differences? Because we are in this mess together?

During these ups and downs, lockdown, reopening, living in Bermuda or dreaming in Wonderland, line-ups for light or living in our fenced world, the only way of approaching anyone was by call, chat, or email, and strangely slow and surreal. I don't know if other people gave up on communication in the virtual world like me or not, but it was the only way, and now and then, we should use it, anyway. However, sometimes organizer approaches were painful.

This second dose vaccination news was so strong that some people believed the trouble was over and they could go out and live normally, even without masks. But after a few times, they noticed with or without masks, the life we had was not coming back. At least, not that easy. In this advertising and messed up life, I decided to get my second dose. I thought we were dying, anyway, with or without the vaccine. How about give it a shot? My second dose had been booked the time I got my first dose with four months in between, but the day after, we heard second doses are available everywhere and everyone could get it. That's why, after around two months, I thought I could save two months of my life by receiving my second dose earlier, but these thoughts soon changed to sitting on the computer for long periods of time checking for any available appointment, and it took another month till I could reschedule my appointment. On that day, I thought this is a big milestone in my life, worth paying tens of dollars for Lyft to get there, and with motivation and hoping for that narrow light, stepped out of my apartment and got to the location. Surprisingly, I noticed a long line up, but it didn't matter, I had booked my appointment and waited for it for three months. I thought I planned and scheduled my life and proudly told volunteers I have an appointment today. In response, not only did I not get to my turn, but also I was yelled at; that they are trying to help me and I have to wait in a long line up, no matter if I am a walk-in or I have an appointment. I understood they were politely asking me shut up and say no more. After a while waiting, finally I got my dose and came out of the clinic. While I was coming home, I watched other people to see if this time anything has changed, but no, it was the same story. Those with cars were sitting without masks and no matter how long this epidemic took, they could travel, go to places, stay together without masks, and the rest should wear masks and wait in line, hoping and praying for a day this narrow light would get bigger.

 Some people after getting their second doses became brave and started partying, dining in, and took their families and kids outside. Some people still couldn't get over this fear that impacted their life and personalities. Interestingly, most of those reactions were psychological because no one even knew if this virus was really killing, or if those who died under the label death with COVID had other unknown diseases, or perhaps died from fear and isolation or lack of physical connections with other human beings. Therefore, it was good. This advertising made some people try to come out of their fences, but we were in the middle of this big news and hoping to get out of Bermuda, which again, was more lockdown news in some areas and more restrictions on borders and entering and existing territories. In this moment, I ran to the narrow light and tried to listen if I could hear anything from outside leaders, but unfortunately, it seemed they were scared too, and for making sure their fencing area was protected, decided to keep us in the underground world for a little bit more.

News of reopening and locking up repeated over and over and over, and it was followed by other news about boosting vaccinations and how everyone should have a vaccination proof card and passport. That news led us to think about a new version of this lifestyle, and we suspected if there wasn't any virus in the first place and it was a methodology for protecting our fences or perhaps staying in Bermuda isolated, and did not expect more about what this and that has and we don't.

It must be something behind this reopening and closing over and over and over and preventing people to travel, eating in restaurant, having parties, making fear of dying, and encouraging us to stay in the underground, and it couldn't be just the COVID virus. How many times in history have we had a world-wide killing virus that makes people be disconnected? Then I thought it could be a type of living in a virtual world test, and then after our generation was sacrificed and was tested with this isolation and living in Bermuda, those who created this situation will find a way to make a balance for the future, if their future could get back to normal, which with what I observed, I doubt it.

Months after months passed, however we were hoping a magic or miracle would happen and life would get back to normal, but it didn't happen. Reopening led to permitting dining in, buying what was not categorized as unnecessary merchandise or luxury needs, watching a movie, and getting together in outside areas, and it was what we all had earned after a long time isolation. Some people jumped on the first opportunity they got for gathering, but again, it couldn't be for all, because some people were living alone or without families and gathering for them meant they had to go to public places like festivals, concerts, sport stadiums, bars, or other places they could meet and hang out with those who had a similar situation, and this reopening drew another line and fence between this group and that group. Interestingly, before the epidemic, no one even knew many groups existed, but after those differences, we realized we were considered second grade citizens for a long time without cars, family, loving relationships, and perhaps a job. When we got to this point, I decided to check the narrow light again to see if outside this hole there was still anyone thinking about this group. The line-up was getting longer and longer. It was showing my group of people are increasing either because of this situation they are losing their cars, families, friends, and jobs, and even places they used to hang out, or another group for protecting their belongings paid lower income group stand in the line-up and keep informing them. In either way, I didn't have anyone else to hope for me. I ran to that light and listened, dreaming to hear from outside that they are trying to resolve this pandemic and take us out before we got stuck in an underground world forever, but surprisingly, we noticed those discussions were getting weaker, like their voice was coming from far, far away. It was somehow scary. Did it mean they gave up on us? Are we stuck in a virtual world and can't get out? I remember there was a movie I was watching when I was a kid in which a group of people were stuck on an unknown planet and their sizes were changed from a normal size to the size of a pen. OMG, we not only should live in a virtual world for the rest of our life, but also we gradually will shrink. That's why we don't need too much space for living, large stages, bigger entertainment places, stores, and even restaurants. We could live with a huge number of people in a room and use our teacup for sleeping and our cattle for partying, wedding and funeral gatherings, those thoughts were more dangerous than this virus. I grabbed the rope in the end of the hole and climbed. I started to screaming help, help, someone help us, but not only did no noise come out of outside, but I noticed everyone in the line-up looking at me like I was crazy and dangerous. At this moment, I realized not everyone has the capacity of knowing what is really happening.

While we were waiting to hear something from outside and busy fighting for our territories, we heard some competition was on by leaders. In a confusing moment, we thought in this underground life we already had competition; spying, copying and jealousy. What is this new competition coming from outside? It was a new scenario that Bermuda living is taking over every territory, and if something happens, we will be completely denied inside each fencing and will blame this and that. We were all living in a loop making a new episode, taking on some victim and simply escaping from consequences by blaming another territory. This way, we gradually forgot any crime, negligence or wrongdoing has punishment. We were moving backward to cave living and anyone who was stronger, richer, more powerful or equipped could slowly take over other rights, and this new competition was a new excuse for them to show how their power and money could make living easier. Somehow, they were showing they were related to outside competition and no one knew if it was true, or if it was another method for expanding their territories. How long more should we live in underground? This fire was expanding more, and in its way, was burning many basic principles and values. People care less about who hurts or whose life is damaged. Everyone was trying to create some type of new story or lies to get to another side of fences, or even to go on the ground. In these unequal tests and errors, I was thinking, now that outside leaders are competing, is it a new beginning for expanding territories on the ground? How long should we wait for someone to notice we need help, and instead of this dangerous inside war, we should sit and discuss what went wrong and how we could correct it, but the only thing I could do was climb to the light, which fortunately was getting bigger and bigger.

Compared to a long time ago, when we all fell in the hole, many things had been changed from building our groups, fencing them, eating on our table with all types of food that we earned or stole, fighting against those who might be a danger for our family, rejecting lonely people, spying and copying, and this list was going on and on., but now some changes are happening. We have a narrow light, a line-up, a hope for a vaccine, a new outside competition, and it seemed most groups had settled down and adopted the virtual world in Bermuda. During this process, we lost Wonderland, bunnies disappeared, we spent less time drinking tea and forced ourselves to believe this nonsense gathering in zoom and the virtual world was entertaining, and prayed. At least they are real and not recorded from years ago, or from another time zone, or how if they are coming from another planet? After all those thoughts, we got back to the underground, sitting on our coach, waiting for a digital connection, and pretended we were the most fortunate people in this new life. Something was very interesting and satisfactory; we were vaccinated, some businesses were reopened, some real or fake connections were made, some new methodology was placed, but we deep down knew they were not the solutions, and we were still suffering from not having family and friends, not going to parties, and not sitting on the beach or swimming in our pool. It was long, long time we had adopted to live alone and talk to Alexa, Bixby, and perhaps Google assistance, so that even we didn't know how we were supposed to react to a real person, and this way, we were witnessing our past lives disappearing one by one. Not only there was not any new relationships out of the virtual world, but those we had moved away far from the present. I thought, really, we are disappearing in Bermuda and those airplanes, ships and boats or hardware that lost probably went through the same situation we did, and since I didn't feel any hope, I grabbed my teacup and ran to the kettle to pour myself another tea. It was the only thing left.

In this situation, what was disturbing was watching those who pretended they had traveled to their younger age or a decade or century earlier , and this way were trying to keep themselves young and get back what they lost. It was creating a new theory in which we can travel in time and go back and change our past, but not only time had already passed and there was no way to get it back, but this nonsense theory caused us to lose three dimensions, specifically time and location dimensions. That's why people were acting weird; some elderly people were acting like kids, some kids pretended they are your parents, and some authorities traveled to a time they hadn't any responsibility, and this way, practically we were melting in this theory without thinking time is moving forward, and it doesn't matter if we pretend we are younger, kids, or even our grandparents. The past is not fixed and time is not stopping.

In one of the epidemic days after reopening, I decided to take my laptop and go to the coffee shop down the street to observe what was going on and get out of this long isolation and living in the virtual world. While I was walking to my destination, I noticed a few people were outside. Usually in this time of day and this season many people were outside as well as coffee shops, but not today. The street was empty and those who bravely were outside were celebrating their victory by not wearing masks, but I wore my mask to make sure in a very dangerous situation I was obeying everything that makes us safe, and I guess it ended up with wearing masks and staying home. I thought I already broke the first one and I am out after reopening, but it's better to stay with my mask. The plaza was not busy; however many businesses were open and their lights were on, but they barely had customers. In coffee shops, there were a few people drinking coffee and mostly they were families, but for some reason, this fencing was in place here, too. I guess either it was my mask or my single status which was not part of their fencing. That's why as soon as I got to the coffee shop and sat to write, they left.

Remaining were single men or boys with friends. I guess most of the girls and women preferred to stay home and in their territory to make sure no one was breaking into their surroundings. In this situation, no one knew if they should go to the salon, spa, photo shoots, or even places that before this epidemic no one even thought about, or stay home, but we all knew we were allowed to eat or take out foods and it was the main reason we were all gaining weight. The good news gyms were reopened, but as I guessed, most of us got used to laying on our coach and chatting in zoom or WhatsApp, besides, it was very good news for working from home without limitation, and any delay or missing work somehow was related to the epidemic and it was better we stay home just in case anyone asked us why jobs are not done. We say we had COVID and this vaccination is not working and demandingly ask the government to pay for the country's emergency, or perhaps world emergency, and pay more to those brave employees who are working in the front line.

I was thinking, if this coffee shop wasn't down my street, without car, probably I was receiving another ticket from an officer who was sacrificing his life to check bus tickets, to make sure the allocated budget to bus and public transportation was not wasted, and with those ticket payments, we have more roads and highways for those who have cars and drive everywhere to stay safe and sound.

This year we even had no voting stations in our area, because apparently, those who don't have cars and live in small condos are carrying the worst virus, and Vote collectors prefer to go to places that have bigger houses, and people drive to voting stations. This way, they could save sanitizer costs and stay in their zooming areas.

Today, a new experience made me instead of running to my teapot, sit on my table, drink my coffee, and feel we are still alive and could breathe the same air everyone else is breathing, regardless of their race, gender, sexuality, and nationality, and it was a good feeling after a long time living on my computer and talking to my smart TV. Then, I thought, is really that narrow light expanding and is it any hope we could get back to normal? How about this new outside competition? Is it a new hope and somehow related to an unknown situation? While I was thinking about those scenarios, I noticed still spies were doing a great job monitoring me and what I am doing to make sure I am not in contact with anyone, and no one is approaching me because apparently, if you are single and a writer, you are in the high danger category, and every other group should monitor your every move, or you should pay and share whatever makes you alive, or you are pushed to the red zone which is marked for those who carry this killing virus against the virtual world and are trying meet face to face or socializing.

In the coffee shop, the light is on, the smell of coffee is good, and looking at the menu board with all types of sandwiches reminded me of a normal life in our small fencing. Isn't that why just a few people are here at this time and date? Because we already turned to small people like that movie and melted into bigger more powerful groups under control, and they are allowed to step on us? Suddenly, I noticed those thoughts were the result of staying a long time under a mask and being careful not to open my mouth, and that's why I decided to walk to the coffee shop more often, take my mask off, and write with others who were here, but soon it turned to regret because of powerful, richer group controls.

One day, I managed to go to the light and climb to see what was happening in the light. I could see and hear leaders having gatherings, talking and planning about how and when they can take us out of Bermuda, everyone suggesting a plan, but I like one of them better. However, it was a long way to go. It wasn't any place to stay in the light, and there wasn't anybody to even notice you, but at least it was a hope. Some groups were trying to take us out of this mess. I had to get back to my place in Bermuda and couldn't stay in the light too long, simply because I didn't belong to that group. That's why I released my hands and slipped on the hole, but as soon as I got back, many of those who were wearing masks suddenly looked at me like I was the biggest threat to them. I ran to my apartment and closed the door, thinking, when everyone is wearing masks, how could we know who is whom, and how mutes and deafs can understand what someone else is saying or planning, and then I figured out that was the main reason for wearing mask in the first place that no one could understand what was said or discussed.

I had noticed before that there were some types of sign language between fencing groups, but I couldn't understand why they didn't talk and use sign language? For a moment, I reviewed history and got back to the time that languages were initiated and the reason behind not understanding other languages.

I Inside fences, everyone knows what is said. It could be the first and apparently the last reason in the twenty-first century why we are not supposed to understand discussion outside of our fencing.

This face masking was getting more and more mysterious and it was making me think more about why we were in this underground, and we got back to caving life and our only communication is the virtual world. Are we really in danger of the virus, or it is another version of epidemic we are not aware of? I mean, we are in danger of getting something, but not for sure a disease. It must be getting some type of unknown danger, which makes outside leaders get together and talk and discuss what is happening and why and when we fell down into this hole, but something I couldn't understand was how come, it took that long for them to get to this point. Obviously, when we were falling down, we felt pain, fear, and some types of transferred troubles, and now, after we have already initiated sign language, fencing, masking and our community and groups have learned to make things that are needed, outsiders are discussing to save us? What is going to happen if we get out and we can't communicate with each other because we used to talk and listen only to our groups? What if this defending mechanism against singles and couples continues out of Bermuda? Isn't that the reason our Wonderland was replaced with Bermuda in the first place? How about spying and digging in other groups' living situation? This motivation will disappear once we live all together out of the underground. In this time, I didn't know if we should be more concerned about living in Bermuda or being saved by outsiders.

While I was laying down on my coach, I tried to review what we had and missed, what has been changed, and which groups are seen more than ever in this epidemic. For some strange reason, I noticed most people I have been facing from the beginning of this epidemic are those who prefer to stay in smaller groups and speak their languages and share their homes and jobs with their groups. For half an hour, I thought, is this the reason I observed a specific race and nationality in fencing groups and even in hospitals and vaccination places? Is it what pushes us in the hole competing with each other for grabbing jobs, income, family and even mates? Are we happier underground? Or are we just satisfied with fencing around our territories and not letting anyone cross the line? Obviously, many are sacrificed here because they don't belong to any group, or simply they don't want to be part of this group against that group.

Since I was one of the lonely people, I decided to get my laptop and run to the coffee shop again to make sure not me nor anyone else who lives alone was left behind in this epidemic, and out of the virtual world we exist, and still there are many other groups who cares for others like me. If we are supposed to stay in this underground another year or years, and God knows, perhaps decades, what is going to happen for those who live in their small fencing without contact because they didn't have time to be part of a family and their types of circles before the pandemic? Should they stay in Bermuda till they die? And even after being saved, still this new culture and approach will stay with us for a long, long time.

Counting the number of lockdowns and re-openings was out of hand, I couldn't keep up with them, but it was almost twenty months after the beginning of this virus that we heard after the second vaccinations, most places were reopened. When I stepped out of my apartment and building, it looked a little bit like before the epidemic, but of course, most travelers were those who were driving. Getting on the bus was just as usual, except a few people more than before were on the bus. Something fascinating about this new situation was the numbers of noticeable white cars compared to other colors. It made me think, does it mean this virus exists and like our body, which creates more white globule when we are sick to protect our body, those white cars are protecting around the living area? For a moment, I laughed at my thoughts, but still I was curious to see what was behind this white movement.

After news had announced a large percentage of the population were vaccinated, malls got busy, in the food court and restaurants, we were asked for proof of vaccination. In this new reopening, with people's excitement for what has not changed, we were ready to adopt any lifestyle no matter if it is underground living, breathing lonely inside our apartment, dreaming about life in the virtual world, or sitting, waiting for someone to save us. That's why I got back to the narrow light again to see what was going on and looked at the long line-up, but interestingly, even in this line-up, they did not know what they were looking for, I thought they just followed the first one stood in the line, without knowing why or how they should stand in line up. They tried to accuse anyone who was trying to climb as she was leaving their safe, comfortable, healthy environment, and was escaping to their neighbors' territories.

It was another sign we really were adoptable and no matter with or without the virus, we should stay and say nothing or we are enemy who is trying to get inside other fences. While I was coming back to inside my fence, I was thinking about how long more we should believe what we have is the best, and no one says anything against limitations and underground living, and if someone tries to make them aware, is labeled as outsider? During my walking, I noticed people were wearing masks and some of them with two layers to make sure not a word was coming out of their mouth to be labeled as someone who is climbing to other territories. Then, I remembered those times rabbits were jumping up and down, and why they were not showing up anymore. Perhaps their movement was a sign of outsiders, and since they were very smart, took Wonderland and left us to stay in our fencing or stand in line, and instead of anything else, just accuse each other and make sure not an unacceptable word was coming out of our lips.

This type of thinking was somehow amazing how still after two years we are searching for someone to blame and cover what we were warned about and ignored. With this new thinking and movement, we made sure anyone staying in the underground forgets how we fell down the hole, when pulled fencing, started cave living, or how long ago we used to have many things. I was very sure in a few months or another year when we will be celebrating going out of our building and breathing, we will not talk about any lighting or on the ground leaders' discussions to make sure we are allowed to live like insiders.

I was wondering, in the creation of heaven, was Adam considered an outsider and Eve an insider? That's why Eve tried to send Adam out of heaven, or it is what we non-religious people are hearing and exactly like this unknown virus is a deeper story behind that. In either way, I got back to sitting on my couch and trying not to think about Wonderland and rabbits and just drinking my tea and being happy that I can walk to a coffee shop in this dangerous virus environment.

However, after the second vaccination, it looked like people were in less fear, many businesses were reopened and the street was busier than before, but on Thanksgiving, when I stepped out of my apartment and walked around a circle by three km diameter, it was like I was in the dead zone. A few people were outside. I tried to believe the rest were eating dinner with their family and I was one of those groups without family and relationships, but no, it wasn't about that. I remembered those Thanksgivings where we were going to coffee shops and there were all types of people with family and without, but this year was different. Those in a group of two or more were walking like they were winners of this situation, and if they couldn't win over the virus, they proudly could keep company with more than one lonely person.

Since the beginning of this epidemic and during lockdown, , most of us were ordering groceries and needed products online, but it was another situation impacted by the virus that I never could get all my groceries in one order without missing items. After vaccination, I thought I could personally go to the store and shop, but getting on the bus, getting a cab, waiting in the line and even payments by credit all were impacted by the epidemic, it was impossible to do a simple grocery like before without barriers or hiding from staring eyes and their blaming looks. That's why I tried to walk around to find a grocery store close to me, but this task in Thanksgiving was the biggest crime in the world I could feel questioning eyes on me how dare you walking lonely while those who have family are celebrating.

It was very annoying, but it was a long time we used to live inside our fences and blame all our bad attitudes, and delays on

Pandemic, and putting our priorities on top of the world list. Therefore, I walked and tried not to listen to their thoughts.

An interesting part of this outside visit was watching the birds traveling in a group, but I wasn't sure they were coming back after the vaccination or leaving. I know before the epidemic they were traveling to warm areas before fall and winter cold weather, but this year, even their immigration was different. No one knows if the virus impacted them or not, and if they got vaccinations or if they are traveling in a group to escape from this fencing and surrounding environment, or perhaps were looking for rabbits from height in the sky. For me, just watching them was sign of life exists, and if we are in the dead zone on the Earth or underground they are alive in the sky.

After hours walking around, drinking a coffee in an empty coffee shop, and not finding any ·stores, I got back to my apartment thinking it is going to get better and hoping outside discussions got somewhere and we will be rescued soon. Then I looked at my teapot and coffee cup and remembered there was a rabbit sitting in my cup, but now the tea was cold and the rabbit had disappeared and it was around two years we had been locked down. Before I feel sad, I jumped in my kitchen, lit up my oven, and tries to get ready for drinking another cup of tea and pray this Christmas without a car I could attend in some gathering instead of watching families with cars celebrating the New Year in drive-through decorated Christmas places on the TV, and thinking, aren't we part of this society? While I was in that thought, I heard a sound of boiling water in my kettle and I totally forgot about the virus, epidemic, and even missing items from my groceries. It was another day of drinking tea, searching for digital meetups, sitting on a balcony watching the sky and pretending everything is perfectly fine.

The situation was getting better slowly. Either outside discussions had got somewhere or those living on the ground were tired of waiting and thinking, what is this situation and how did we all get here, and they decided to take a risk and open some of the fences and advertise situations as safe for living a normal life, but unfortunately it was not. Anytime I stepped out of my building to discover more, I noticed people were more sensitive to anyone who was writing or thinking, and they all act like you are a criminal who reports their hiding and taking advantage of the situation, but the truth was, they were in fear and elders were scared to death and even we were hearing many of them died. That's why they were looking for someone to blame, to feel better with themselves, and who is better than a writer or thinker? They are always good targets. You can critique, question, or even roast them, and no one asks you what the hell that was.

Something they couldn't realize, those who were targets for blaming were looking for light and waiting in a line-up to find a way, and they knew how living in Bermuda might lead to disappearance. I was thinking, is it normal that we blame someone else for our failures and falling down in the hole? Wasn't this the main reason the rabbits were not with us anymore and we lost Wonderland? But whatever the reason, was, it was better they hide behind their masks and pretend others were responsible for what they were going through, sat back in their adopted life and wait for the same target they threw their fault on to find a way to save us.

Regardless of what each group was thinking, the situation was improving from nothing to having something and it was good news no matter if your home fence was shorter than others and others could throw their garbage in your yard. As much as this lockdown was depressing and closed many opportunities, it had some bright sides, like many people who did not even touch computers before, suddenly they were chatting and communicating through computers, or the same parents who were preventing their kids from sitting on the computer all day were encouraging them to sit and read, play, communicate, and do whatever on their computers and cell phones, just they should stay home, and of course developers were sending app after app to the market which was the best part of the pandemic. It was like you were traveling all over the world in your imagination while are sitting on your coach jumping from this app to that app. I remember a book about a brave creative person who had traveled over the world in eighty days, and while I was smiling, I thought how fast our life moves from a story about a trip that amazed a generation to sitting in my apartment to watch, talk, read, communicate and learn from another side of the world. In this isolated time, personally I could discover many hidden sides of the world, but there was no doubt we had lost our three dimensions of our life. It was interesting how for decades, scientists, engineers, and doctors had tried to improve tools into three dimensions. That's why we have 3D printers or 3D movies, and 3D artificial organs, but now we are sitting in our apartments and our only dimensions of our life are digital and the COVID virus. No contact from another person, no travel, no live entertaining, and no gathering and they caused us to have no real life, family and live alone.

    Then I thought, when my only option is the digital world, it's better I use it before losing it. I jumped on my computer and started to search for something as limited pandemic culture and environment was dictated that it should be age, gender and race appropriate, and even in my personal life, I am not allowed to use available tools without limitations. In this mixed excitement and annoying search, I discovered some socializing, communicator and connection apps which I could spend my time on, and finally a gathering, of course in my age range, so I could hang out with new friends.

They opened a new door from living underground to a narrow light, but because of long fencing, it came with some obstacles and I was hoping they would improve like our 3D tools and prayed it wouldn't stop like our 3D life. Another piece of good news was borders started to reopen and it was a sign of outside discussions were getting somewhere. However, we were improving in this new life style, but deep down we all knew we lost years of life just because we wanted to live inside our fences, keep our family away from possible threat, tried to show we are better than our neighbors, compete with other groups, and blame our failures and took advantage of their success and doubt of fighting with this killing unknown virus, which after years, still no one knew what it was and where it began, except high knowledgeable medical experts who believed they know what they were doing.

In this situation, how much I was thinking more I could understand less. I decided to stay with my coffee shop, my teapot, new gathering groups and my apps and hide my disappointment and years of wasted life by writing. Something I couldn't understand was who put this age limitation on using apps. Obviously they were built for anyone's use and I am sure no one said if your gender, age or nationality is this, you could not use that. If it had restriction, we wouldn't have access to them in the first place. Obviously any product has marketing based on audiences and some groups usage are higher than others in any product, but was not supposed tricking and trying to spy on other users for their age, sex orientation, nationality, or other differences categorized as discrimination, stereotyping and racism? Then I realized this is "something is better than nothing, and no questions should be asked situation. Suddenly I felt I was in army and I should obey the "don't ask don't tell" rule.

I felt very clever with this analysis and found those who were spying, checking, lying, hiding and monitoring what and why someone is doing against what they are not doing, eating, using or even talking is the main reason of fencing, masking, and living underground, and perhaps I should be careful on the street, in the store or in the digital world. There might be very dangerous people around who are trying to take over my teapot or my zoom gathering, or even worse than that our live gathering. When I got to this point I realized it is another unknown reason beside unknown COVID, I laugh at this game everyone is playing detective after we all are falling down, then this happy feeling makes me hungry and I have to give myself a cup of tea and plate of food as only rewards in COVID situation.

After two years, evidence around was telling this epidemic almost was over. Most businesses were opened, streets were not as empty as before, and it seemed people were in less fear and news was announced over and over we could get back to our normal life, but when I was walking in this underground, attending limited available in-person gatherings, trying to communicate with others, talking to those who I knew before this spreading virus or even trying to find a new hobby, it was very clear we are facing with huge changes. I decided to take a long walk in this Bermuda living and look at this situation from the beginning to this point, hoping to find what this virus is, and suddenly this light shine in my head and a small light lit up inside my brain and I thought I got it.

Covid-19 was over, but what was this in the first place? I

reviewed all situations and I got to the point, that the main reason for this Pandemic was a difference in our basic definition. Before this situation, we all were sharing some definition, values, and principles, such as what is beautiful and ugly, how a student should behave, who is issuing orders in society and inside homes, who is holding power, and who is making rules, what is every group responsibility or obligation, and why we are taught to use this word in this place and not that place, and other basic definitions in technical terms we plan once, but we schedule and reschedule every task many times.

It was the moment I knew what was going on. Our basics had been changed while we were living on the ground in our normal life and it was the main reason we all fell down in the hole. We were forced to change our priorities from focusing on groups who are respected to not respected, and changing definitions of sexy, power, safety, colors, who is responsible for what, who is issuing orders and making rules, and who should obey. Definitions of popular, high income, high power, and every basic in our life had been changing and it was what once was planned by an unknown group.

It was the beginning of this virus which was called disease. The plan replaced all our acceptable basics with a new series of tasks that were linked together. That's why all schools and universities were closed, huge companies released their high position employees, well-known businesses such as banks, lawyers, courts, and management offices were taken to lower levels in society, learning, gathering and talking were forbidden, and we were asked to wear masks and cover most of our face not to be seen. Instead of conferences and speeches we had been listening to jokes and humor targeting our previous basics. Working, which was one of our values, changed from an active exciting goal to sitting inside our fences and waiting for our pay check from government budgets. Everything we someday were enjoying, replaced with listening to others' sadness and problems. Gyms were closed and changed with more eating and gaining weight. Taking showers and smelling good was replaced with not being clean, and every single definition we knew changed and it was a plan which once had been designed, and during two years lockdown, has been scheduled.

It was a moment where I discovered the resolution to the biggest problem in the world, and now I could see all my answers in front of me. How we all were scared to step out of our home, how those on the front lines got all the attention and other groups were closed. Change in our baseline made any group except front line be blamed and questioned for every outfit, exercise, learning, conference, education, gathering, shopping, doing groceries, taking showers, going to salons, traveling and working, and those who were responsible for helping, serving and protecting were given permission to take a side.

With all this plan, we were pushed into this hole to adopt these new definitions and it was the beginning of masking which was called pandemic; it was a good name as it was spread all over the world, extended to borders, the economy, banking and stocking systems, country leaders, and gradually, every definition of who is first, who is the best, who is holding power, what is the best city or education system in the world, who should obey whom, who should have a family, marriage, kids and who are not allowed, who and what is priority and who is not, who should work and who should stay home, and every single value and principle, changed and not only impacted inside the hole, but also affected those in the light and outside underground. That's why no one knew what this was and their efforts for isolation, masking, keeping people inside their homes, preventing working and going to school, traveling, and anything they thought was a good way for fighting with this virus, in reality was expanding the plan. They were putting something in place and after a while, they revised it because the plan has been scheduling and rescheduling.

Finally, this situation and disease were not unknown anymore. I sat on my couch and took a deep breath to know being a target of fencing, fears, and losing family and friends did not have unknown reasons. They were planned, and even we could get out of this hole and we are not disappearing like Bermuda victims. However, we have been forced to adopt new definitions and anything against those plan cause a new labeling and pressure. It was the end of this COVID-19 story, deep down, I knew it was impossible; a virus taking over all the world. With this new understanding, the economy, politics, and even identities were changed, and they were not just for one area or fencing, it was included in anything and every fencing inside and outside, and we are victims of this plan. Regardless of how we were pushed into this hole or we get out of this life, still many adopted new definitions melted in our culture s for those kids who were little before and now are in their teenage years, younger who are in adulthood, and of course, those who are born after the pandemic, and perhaps it was the reason many elderlies died because they weren't allowed to remember old definitions, rules, and principles or who is responsible for what.

It was a hard, unbelievable and unpleasant experience, but at least now I knew, sitting on the couch losing rabbits and Wonderland, sticking with my teapot, wearing masks, not attending in-person gatherings or facing friends and family, and hearing nonsense in the digital world, everything was planned and it was called COVID-19; however, I was a witness of losing all our values and principles, definitions, and even identity. Standing in a long line, climbing to the light and living in a virtual world was the best I could do.

It was the end of the pandemic, at least for me, after two years regardless of the result that was dictated by planners and schedulers, but I knew we will be suffering from the side effects of this disease for generations.

CPSIA information can be obtained
at www.ICGtesting.com
Printed in the USA
LVHW040001120623
749203LV00001B/9